Beckett Blaise

Journal of a Vampire

Shrouded in Shadows

As Journaled by Sabastian Wolfram, a Vampire

Shadesilver Publishing

Join in on the fun!

My newsletter has free books, sales on books, exclusive deals, and more. You can also get the latest news on my new releases! Just scan the QR code below.

Shrouded in Shadows: A Vampire's Journal

Copyright © 2025 by Beckett Blaise

All rights reserved.

No part of this book may be reproduced in any form or by any electronic or mechanical means, including information storage and retrieval systems, without written permission from the author, except for the use of brief quotations in a book review.

This is a work of fiction. Names, characters, businesses, places, events, and incidents are either the product of the author's imagination or are used fictitiously. Any resemblance to actual persons, living or dead, events, or locals is entirely coincidental

Contact info: author.beckettblaise@gmail.com

Front Cover Design by Shadesilver Publishing.

Print Cover Design by Shadesilver Publishing.

Editor: Mark E. Tyson

SECOND EDITION : APRIL 2025

10 9 8 7 6 5 4 3 2 1

Beckett Blaise

Shrouded in Shadows

As journaled by Sabastian Wolfram, a Vampire

———•———⟨∞⟩———•———

A Companion Book to the
Novel
That Bastard the Vampire

Shadesilver Publishing

CONTENTS

Introduction	1
1. Chapter 1: Chapter 1 Introduction of a Vampire	3
2. Chapter 2: From the Writings of Denholm Smith, Vampire Hunter, Rose and Raven Society: Entry 1	7
3. Chapter 3: It is in Our Nature	10
4. Chapter 4: From the Writings of Denholm Smith, Vampire Hunter, Rose and Raven Society: Entry 2	15
5. Chapter 5: Vampire Society	17
6. Chapter 6: From the Writings of Denholm Smith, Vampire Hunter, Rose and Raven Society: Entry 3	22
7. Chapter 7: The Hunt	27
8. Chapter 8: From my own writings. My first Vampire Hunter Encounter.	31
9. Chapter 9: The Hunter Being Hunted	35
10. Chapter 10: From the Writings of Denholm Smith, Vampire Hunter: Entry 4	40
11. Chapter 11: Vampires Hunting Humans	45

12.	Chapter 12: From the Report of Sheriff Jose Jimenez: Entry 6	50
13.	Chapter 13: The Curse: Becoming a Vampire	54
14.	Chapter 14: From the Writings of Eliza Blount: Fledgling Vampire Entry 7	59
15.	Chapter 15: Vampire Relationships	61
16.	Chapter 16: From the Writings of Lunare and Selene: Vampire Lovers Entry 8	65
17.	Chapter 17: Vampire Communities	67
18.	Chapter 18: From the Writings of Sabastian Wolfram: The Desert Moon of the Sahara Entry 9	72
19.	Chapter 19: Our Ways: Vampire Abilities	75
20.	Chapter 20: From the Writings of a Fledgling Vampire discovered in a journal in an abandoned hotel room: Entry 10	80
21.	Chapter 21: Our History	84
22.	Chapter 22: An account of my meeting Bram Stoker and the vampire Sir Henry Irving in the early 1900s – Sabastian Wolfram	88
23.	Chapter 23: Rogue Vampires	90
24.	Chapter 24: From the Writings of Ebenezer Smith, Vampire Hunter, Rose and Raven Society 1791	95
25.	Chapter 25: Famous Vampire Hunter Accounts	100

26.	Chapter 26: Journal Entry of John Stanley: Famous Vampire Hunter– November 3, 1896	105
27.	Chapter 27: Vampire Legends	107
28.	Chapter 28: Personal Encounter, Sabastian Wolfram – April 23, 1927	112
29.	Chapter 29: Our Survival	114
30.	Chapter 30: What I Know About this Vampire Named Sabastion Wolfram So Far – by Beckett Blaise	118

Introduction
Shrouded in Shadows

This journal was passed to me by a man named Seth Aubrey. Although I don't know what became of the man, I understand he was once the biographer of the vampire author in question. He left this journal with me because of my affiliation with the Rose and Raven Society, an ancient organization dedicated to the investigation and adjudication of the unknown and the unnatural. I have authenticated it with the archives of the Rose and Raven Society. There is a record with the name Sabastian E. Wolfram and given that if the E stands for Elijah can be confirmed this journal's author is the vampire on file with the society.

There is a rumor about a manuscript titled "That Bastard the Vampire: An Unauthorized Biography" by Seth Aubrey. I shall endeavor to find this manuscript and publish it as well. I am currently working with a couple of agents of the society to find Seth Aubrey, but I fear the worst for him. It seems the 'gentle' nature of the vampire Wolfram might have been an exaggeration on his part. His claim within this journal that he never kills might not be as accurate as one might hope.

The struggles of Mr. Aubrey with his vampire subject, it is my hope, are chronicled in his unauthorized biography. As I have stated, I fear the worst for Mr. Aubrey, especially if his scathing writings about Mr. Wolfram offended. I suppose we will see when I find the fabled manuscript. In the meantime, here is the journal of Sabastian Wolfram. He is wanting us, the reader, to sympathize with him. I would recommend caution, for he is a vampire, and I do not truth any of them.

When I read through this journal, I noticed many, many contradictory entries and statements. This vampire is one of the worst liars I have come across. I don't think he even tried to keep all his stories and timelines straight. Read every entry in this journal with skepticism. Note: Although I believe many entries fabrications, every entry contains scraps of the truth. The discerning hunter and field agent can read between the lines and see the patterns of truth about the real Sabastian Wolfram.

Beckett Blaise – Vampire Expert: Rose and Raven Society

Chapter 1
Introduction of a Vampire

My name is Sabastian Elijah Wolfram, and I am a vampire. I realize that for most, vampires have been the stuff of myths. Our existence has been relegated to the pages of gothic novels and the flickering glow of movie screens. But what if I told you that vampires are not merely figments of imagination? What if I revealed that we walk among you, hidden in plain sight, our existence meticulously concealed by centuries of secrecy and careful manipulation?

Let me start by explaining what it means to be a vampire. Forget the clichés of capes, fangs, and sleeping in coffins. Those are exaggerations created to mock and mystify the truth. Vampirism is a curse and a transformation, a redefinition of life itself. A vampire is a being who has transcended mortality, trading the constraints of human existence for something more enduring, more powerful—and, yes, more isolating.

We are creatures of the night, not because sunlight turns us to ash, but because the day belongs to the living. Our senses are heightened, sharper than any human could imagine. We see in the dark as clearly as others see in daylight. We hear whispers across crowded rooms and smell emotions like fear and desire. Our strength and speed surpass human limitations, and our bodies heal with a speed that defies logic. But this power comes at a cost: the unrelenting need for blood. It is not the act of drinking it that sustains us, but the life force within it. Without it, we weaken, wither, and eventually fade.

Now, let me share how I came to know this truth.

It happened two years ago on a night that began like any other. I was walking home late, the streets eerily quiet, the air heavy with the scent of rain. My life up until that moment had been unremarkable, a series of mundane routines and unfulfilled dreams. I was no one special, certainly not the kind of person you'd expect to be drawn into the world of the supernatural.

The attack came swiftly, without warning. One moment I was alone, and the next, a figure loomed in the shadows, moving with inhuman speed. Before I could scream, I felt the sharp sting of teeth piercing my neck, followed by a flood of warmth and darkness. I thought I was dying. I was!

When I woke, I was no longer the same. The world around me had shifted, every detail sharper, more vivid. The sounds of the city, once a dull hum, were now a symphony of voices, engines, and footsteps. Hunger gnawed at me, a primal, insatiable need that I couldn't understand until my maker appeared.

He was calm, patient, and terrifyingly beautiful. He explained what had happened, how he had chosen me for reasons he would not yet reveal. He taught me the rules of our kind: never kill when feeding, blend in with humanity, and above all, protect the secret of our existence. To break these rules was to invite destruction, not just for oneself, but for the entire brethren.

Learning to live as a vampire was like being born again into a world I thought I knew. I had to relearn how to interact with people, how to suppress the hunger that surged whenever I was near them. My maker guided me, but his lessons were harsh. He made me hunt, forcing me to confront the reality of what I had become. The first time I fed, I wept for what I had lost—for my humanity, for the life I would never return to. I made a vow that no matter what he chose me for, whether good or bad, I would one day kill him for what he took against my will.

Yet, as the months passed, I began to see the beauty in my new existence. The world opened up in ways I could never have imagined. I moved through it with a grace and confidence that had eluded me in my mortal life. I discovered that while I had lost the ability to walk freely in the sunlight, I had gained something far greater: the freedom to live without fear of time, disease, or death.

Still, the isolation is real. No matter how deeply I bond with my kind, I cannot forget what I once was. Every human I encounter reminds me of the life I left behind. But perhaps that is the point. To be a vampire is to exist on the threshold between life and death, to see the world from both sides and to know that, in the end, we are all connected by the same fragile thread.

Still, the burning inside me to punish my maker persisted. No matter how much I accepted my fate, or even enjoyed it, I still longed to kill him.

So now you know. Vampires are real. We are not the monsters you fear, nor the romantic heroes you idolize. We are something in between, a reflection of humanity's greatest hopes and darkest fears. And we are watching. I have always journaled, and I see no reason to halt the practice. I will keep this book secret until one day, perhaps after I am gone from this world, someone will read these pages and understand my plight and the reasons behind my actions. Just for fun, I will also include within these pages excerpts from confiscated journals of vampire hunters, killers, and others whose paths I have crossed. It is through their observance that you may understand me in even greater detail.

Below, I am including some writings by a man who has stalked me for a large portion of my unnatural life. I found his writings in a hotel room. What became of him I do not know, but please do not accuse me. I would never wish harm upon anyone. It is my hope that through his eyes, you will see me, the real me.

Chapter 2
From the Writings of
Denholm Smith
Rose and Haven Vampire Hunter Entry I

Night 1: I saw him tonight. He was thin, too thin, and pale. I paid close attention to his laughter because when he smiled, he revealed his teeth. They were jagged and not straight as I had thought. The canines were high up on his gums, but I did not detect the long tooth of a fiend such as he is thought to be. He seems to surround himself with women though he does not appear attractive to me at least, but that may be my own bias, for he does seem, no matter how awkward he is socially, to find his way into the arms of the fairer sex. Speaking of his laughter, it is shrill and grating on the ear, likened to a rusty hinge on an unkempt gate. Surely this cannot be the same monster who hunts the hapless, the innocent, and the unaware during the night. He is simple in the mind, forgetful in the soul, and clumsy with his words.

Night 2: From my observations tonight, most of the women he comes in contact with and with whom he tries to carry on a conversation shy away from him. I think the information the fine researchers at the Rose and Raven society have given me is incorrect. This can't be the blood-sucking fiend of whom I have been warned. I will watch him closely though I do feel I am wasting my time.

Night 3: Something is different. He is very well dressed compared to the other nights I have observed him. He is carrying himself differently, more confidently. He looked my way earlier and before I could turn away I made eye contract. It took me a while to shake the feeling. It was eerie yet comforting as if I knew I would be safe in his presence. Once the effect wore off, I knew what was different about him this night. He was getting ready to feed and he was using his powers to charm his way to satiety. The women are acting much different toward him now. They are friendly and welcoming. It is only a matter of time before one walks away with him. I know what will happen to her if she does. I must stay vigilant and watch him. Surely, if he is weakened to the point he needs to feed, he will be too weak to charm both of us. Perhaps I can save whoever he lures.

* * *

Here are some entries I found among his things in the Hotel room. They are some random pages to a journal or diary of a vampire. I think he attributed these to me. Although these entries do seem familiar, they are not in my handwriting so I would not attribute them to me since I wasn't turned until World War II. although they are interesting. I am including them to clear myself of the implication that I may have written them.

Even though he uses my name, I think he has me confused with another vampire. The 1923 entry did give me an idea though. I need to research if what the entry says is true.

April 17, 1794 – I write these words with hands that no longer feel like my own. Three nights have passed since my rebirth, since Lady Eleanor found me walking home from Thornfield Farm and offered me shelter from the storm. I was but a farmer's hand, covered in mud and reeking of livestock. Why she chose me, I cannot fathom...

June 3, 1801 – Seven years of this cursed existence. I did not ask for this life. I did not seek immortality or power. It was thrust upon me by a creature who saw me as nothing more than amusement, then discarded me when I failed to provide adequate entertainment.

November 12, 1923 – I have found a way. The texts speak of an Ascension, a means by which our kind may transcend the limitations imposed upon us. The hunger that never ceases, the weaknesses that plague us, the isolation that stretches through centuries, all might be overcome. If this existence was forced upon me, am I not entitled to better it by any means necessary?

Chapter 3
It is in Our Nature

As I have asserted, vampires are real. I should know—because I am one. As I have mentioned before, we are not the romanticized figures of fiction, nor the grotesque monsters of old myths, at least we are no longer. We are something in between, creatures shaped by biology and necessity, bound by rules and instincts that govern our existence. If you are willing to suspend disbelief, I will tell you what it truly means to be a vampire.

First, let us discuss the Physical and Supernatural Attributes

The transformation from human to vampire changes more than just your dietary needs. It reshapes you, both physically and metaphysically. Our bodies become something more than human, optimized for survival and predation. My skin, for example, is pale and unnaturally smooth, almost luminous in low light. It is cool to the touch, though not corpse-like as some legends suggest. This pallor is a byproduct of the transformation, as the need for oxygen diminishes and our cells are sustained by the life force we draw from blood. I do still benefit from the properties of oxygen it is merely lessened. I can stay underwater for long periods of time for example living off the oxygen present in the water, or underground living off the oxygen in the soil. I would not fare so well in the vacuum of space where there is no oxygen present, although I have never heard of one of my kind doing such a thing so it's merely theoretical.

Our senses are heightened to an extraordinary degree. I can hear a whisper across a crowded room, distinguish the faintest scent of fear, lust, or desire, and see in the dark as clearly as in daylight. These enhanced senses are both a gift and a burden, as the world becomes overwhelming in its detail. The faint hum of electricity, the heartbeat of a passerby, the rustle of leaves in the wind—all of it is amplified, demanding constant focus to filter out the noise.

We are also far stronger and faster than humans, our muscles operating with a precision and power that defy logic. I can lift objects that no human could budge and move so quickly that I appear to blur. These abilities are not limitless, however; they require energy, and energy comes at a cost.

The cost of being one of my kind brings me to the strengths and weaknesses of vampires.

Immortality is our greatest strength and our greatest curse. My body no longer ages, no longer succumbs to disease or the ravages of time. I have healed from injuries that would have been fatal to a human, my wounds closing almost as quickly as they are made. This regenerative ability is one of the reasons we are so difficult to kill.

But we are not invincible. Sunlight, while not instantly lethal, is deeply harmful. Prolonged exposure weakens us, sapping our strength and leaving us vulnerable. We can walk in the daytime, but the effect is the exact opposite of the living. They lie unconscious and vulnerable at night and become weakened when deprived of sleep. We weaken in the day for the same reason. Silver is another weakness, burning our flesh on contact and disrupting our ability to heal. The antibacterial properties and pureness of the metal antagonizes the unnatural state of the undead. And while religious symbols, whether the Holy Cross or the Star of David, have no inherent power, the unwavering faith of the person wielding them can create a psychological barrier that is difficult to overcome. It is the faith behind the symbol.

Perhaps our greatest weakness is our dependency on blood. Without it, we weaken, our bodies withering into a state of torpor—a death-like slumber from which we can only awaken with fresh sustenance. This dependency binds us to the living, making us both predator and parasite. It is a symbiotic state since those we feed on retain the properties of our blood for a time afterward. A willing participant in the feeding ritual without fear can result in some medical miracles such as the curing of cancer or the removal of blood borne pathogens. It is rare to find this symbiotic relationship; however, for fear taints the process and we are feared by humans because of our nature.

Feeding Habits and the Necessity of Blood

Blood is not merely sustenance; it is life itself. When I feed, I am not just drinking liquid. I am drawing the very essence of vitality. This is why animal blood, while sufficient to stave off starvation, is a poor substitute for human blood. It lacks the potency, the vibrancy that we need to truly thrive. Lesser blood is like a snack while human blood is a meal.

The act of feeding is both intimate and predatory. My fangs are sharp, designed to pierce flesh with minimal pain. When I bite, my venom, for lack of a better word for it, dulls the sensation, inducing a state of euphoria in my prey. Most humans do not even realize what is happening until it is over, their memories clouded by the chemical effects of my venom.

I am careful when I feed. I take only what I need, leaving my prey alive and unharmed. To do otherwise would be reckless, drawing attention to our existence. There are rules among vampires, unwritten but universally understood: never kill when feeding, never feed in a way that risks exposure, and always erase the memory of the encounter. To break these rules is to invite the wrath of our kind, and the possibility of discovery by yours. There are notorious vampires who are, or were, predatory killers, but this is nothing new. Your kind is also plagued by the occasional psychopath as well.

The Balance of Existence

Being a vampire is a constant balancing act. Our strengths are tempered by our weaknesses, our immortality by our dependence on the living. We walk a fine line between predator and protector, taking what we need while striving to leave the world untouched by our presence.

I have learned to live with this paradox, to embrace the duality of my existence. I am a creature of the night, but I am also more than that. I am a witness to the passing of time, a guardian of secrets, and a reminder that life is both fragile and enduring.

So, if you ever feel a chill in the darkness or sense eyes watching you from the shadows, remember we are real, we are here, and we are hungry. But we are also bound by the same forces that govern all life: the need to survive, the desire to belong, and the hope that, even in the darkness, we can find a way to coexist.

Chapter 4
From the Writings of Denholm Smith
Rose and Raven Vampire Hunter Entry 11

Night 3 cont. He glamoured me. I don't know how else to put it. He is wise to me following and observing him. I saw him pick up a woman wearing a red dress. At first, I thought the color of her dress would make her conspicuous, but then I realized red might conceal the awful color of blood better than most other colors. He took the woman into the alleyway. I followed only to awaken a few short moments ago. He did something to me to make me not only forget the encounter, but also to fall asleep. Thankfully, I spotted the woman in red on the dance floor acting as if nothing had happened, but I know the truth. I will try to get close to her so I can see if she bears the marks on her neck. They will heal quickly, according to the Rose and Raven field manual I carry with me at all times, but surely the marks have not had adequate time to be completely hidden from view.

Night 3 cont. I boldly asked the woman in red to dance, she accepted. Her hair covered her neck, but I managed to get her to turn her head once and sure enough there was the mark of the vampire. It was already healing. In fact, the two marks were only marginally visible. She only danced with me for one song citing that she was dizzy and tired. I do not doubt for a second. I wonder how much of her blood he siphoned from her.

Night 4: I waited at the club for a couple of hours, but the vampire did not show again. I suspect he was spooked by my presence. He obviously knew I was watching him. I decided to go to the hotel where I suspect he was staying to inquire about him.

Night 4: cont. I talked to the hotel clerk. He did check out this evening. He left no forwarding address. I really didn't expect him to especially if he were suspicious of my presence. I shall endeavor to pick up his trail. It shouldn't be difficult. I was taught by the best and I am not without my own gifts. I will be on his trail before he gets far. I need to freshen my disguise. He will be looking out for me, and I can't have him spotting me so easily.

Chapter 5
Vampire Society

I was thinking this afternight that it might be a good thing to write about how vampire society works. If for no other reason to dispel some of the misconceptions. I do not always intermingle with groups of my kind. That would be a bit like being in the mafia and always having to watch your back. However, I will give an account as best I can.

The Shadow Society

The world you know is a thin veil over a deeper, darker reality. Our existence is hidden, not because we fear humanity, but because we value the delicate balance that allows us to coexist with you unnoticed. Beneath the surface of your bustling cities and quiet towns lies a meticulously organized society of vampires, governed by rules and traditions older than your oldest civilizations.

The Hierarchy of Vampires

Our society is structured like a web, with the Elders at its center. These are the oldest and most powerful of our kind, vampires who have existed for centuries, perhaps millennia. They are the keepers of our history and the architects of our laws. Each Elder presides over a region, ensuring that the vampires within their domain adhere to the rules and maintain the secrecy of our existence.

Beneath the Elders are the Deacons, their enforcers and emissaries. Deacons act as intermediaries between the Elders and the rest of vampire society. They oversee smaller territories within the Elder's domain, resolving disputes and ensuring order. If a vampire steps out of line, it is the Deacon who decides their fate.

At the base of the hierarchy are the common vampires, often referred to as the Kin or Brethren. We are the majority, bound by the laws and expectations set forth by the Elders. Among us, there are further distinctions based on age and skill. Newly turned vampires, or fledglings, are considered the lowest rank until they prove their loyalty and competence. Older vampires, those who have survived centuries, command respect for their experience and power.

Roles in Vampire Society

Our society is not chaotic; it is a finely tuned machine where every vampire has a role to play. Some vampires are hunters, tasked with securing sustenance for the brethren while ensuring discretion. These individuals are skilled in the art of blending in, choosing their prey carefully to avoid suspicion.

Others serve as scholars, chronicling our history and studying the supernatural forces that govern our existence. These vampires are the keepers of knowledge, preserving the secrets of our kind and exploring the mysteries of immortality. We call them Archivists.

There are also warriors trained to protect the brethren from external threats. While conflicts with humans are rare, rivalries between vampire factions can erupt, and warriors ensure that our society remains secure.

Finally, there are diplomats, vampires skilled in negotiation and manipulation. They liaise with human institutions, ensuring that any accidental exposure is swiftly covered up. Diplomats are also responsible for maintaining peace between factions of the brethren, preventing disputes from escalating into full-blown wars.

Rules and Expectations

To be a vampire is to live by a strict code of conduct. Our primary rule is secrecy. The existence of vampires must remain hidden at all costs. This means no reckless feeding, no unnecessary violence, and no leaving evidence that could lead humans to uncover the truth.

Another rule is loyalty to the brethren. Vampires, with a few exceptions, are not solitary creatures; we thrive in communities. Betraying your brethren is considered the gravest sin, punishable by exile or death. Loyalty ensures our survival, as it binds us together against external threats.

Respect for the hierarchy is also paramount. Elders and Deacons are not to be challenged lightly. Their authority is absolute, and their decisions are final. Even among the Kin, respect for age and power is deeply ingrained.

Finally, there is the expectation of restraint. Vampires are predators, but we are also sentient beings. Indulging in unnecessary cruelty or feeding to excess is frowned upon. We are taught to see humans not just as prey but as a vital part of the ecosystem that sustains us. However, if cruel undead did not exist, there would be no laws governing us. Just because we have rules and laws does not mean we do not have those among us who would break them without hesitation. The hunger is real. It is not a good idea to wantonly put your kind's trust into one of my kind. Due diligence is important. After all, you would not immediately trust a stranger of your kind would you.

My Place in the Shadow Society

I am a hunter, a role I did not choose but one I have come to accept. My task is simple: feed without being seen and ensure that no trace of our presence is left behind. It is a lonely job, but it suits me. I have learned to move through the world unnoticed, to read people's desires and fears, to strike and retreat before they even realize what has happened.

But even as a hunter, I am bound by the rules of our society. I report to my Deacon, who monitors my activities and ensures that I remain within the boundaries of our laws. My life is one of discipline and purpose, a far cry from the chaotic existence I once imagined vampires to have.

And yet, there is a strange comfort in this order. Our society, for all its rigidity, has endured for centuries because of its structure. It is this structure that allows us to exist alongside humanity, unseen and unchallenged. I have found my place within it, and though I long for the freedom of my mortal days, I know that this life—this shadowy existence—is my reality now. I have given some though to a biographer, someone of your kind to confide in and to tell my life story to, but I have not yet figured out a way to chronicle my life and keep it secret at the same time. I would assume a human biographer would want to publish his work and make money from it. Who would document my life and not want to publish it?

Anyway, I implore you to be wary of your surroundings especially at night. The next time you walk through a crowded street or sit alone in a dimly lit café, remember we are there, watching, listening, living among you. You may not see us, but we see you. And we will do whatever it takes to ensure that our world and yours remain separate, for both our sakes. Still. I long for the day this journal can be read, or my memoires can be enjoyed. So far, the centuries have not been kind to those who have tried to tell their dark stories.

Chapter 6
From the Writings of Denholm Smith
Rose and Raven Vampire Hunter Entry III

Night 5: I found him. He is going home. This may be it, my big break. I have followed him to the train station, and I paid the ticket master handsomely to tell me where the gentleman is headed. I think he might have been summoned home by the Elders, or at least his deacon. Something big is happening. I can feel it in my bones. No wonder he recently fed. He is on a mission to get home, and he will need the sustenance. At least his victim remained safe. I don't have to contend with the guilt that comes with the belief I might have shared some responsibility in the death of the young girl. I will know to keep my distance from him this time. It seems my old man disguise is holding up. Several men have referred to me as 'old-timer' since we left the railway station.

Night 5 cont. I am in the birth next to him. I will hear if he leaves his room or stirs about on the train. I am going to try to get some shuteye, but I dare not sleep too deeply and I am going to keep one eye opened. I don't think he is suspicious of me, but I would rather not take any chances.

Night 6: I've been watching Wolfram for three days now. He's settled into a routine in this small town. He makes visits to the local library during evening hours, long walks after midnight, and occasional stops at the diner where he orders coffee he barely touches. The waitress there, a pretty blonde named Marlene, blushes whenever he speaks to her. Poor girl doesn't know what kind of monster she's batting her eyelashes at.

Today I spotted him meeting with a nervous-looking fellow carrying a leather portfolio. David Chenowith, I learned later, some sort of writer for the local paper, who's apparently been chronicling Wolfram's "life story." What a joke. The vampire was all charm, clapping the man on the shoulder like they were old friends, but I saw the way Chenowith flinched at his touch.

I followed them to a café and sat close enough to overhear snippets. Wolfram was promising him "unprecedented access" and "stories no one has ever heard." Chenowith looked both terrified and thrilled. The fool has no idea what he's gotten himself into.

Night 7: Made a breakthrough today. After watching Wolfram interact with Chenowith again, I'm convinced the vampire feeds on more than just blood. He seems to draw sustenance from the misery and drama he creates around him. The way he toyed with Chenowith was almost artistic building him up with promises of exclusive material, then casually mentioning he'd spoken to Chenowith's editor about "concerns" regarding his last article.

The color drained from Chenowith's face faster than if Wolfram had sunk his teeth into him. The vampire actually seemed to straighten up afterward, more vibrant, more alive. It was subtle, but I've been hunting his kind long enough to notice these things.

Later, I saw Wolfram chatting with a young woman outside the newspaper office. She turned out to be Chenowith's girlfriend, based on how the writer's face fell when he spotted them together. Wolfram caught his eye across the street and smiled. Not the smile of a predator about to feed, but something worse. The smile of someone who enjoys the game more than the kill.

Night 8: Chenowith's article was pulled from today's paper. I heard him arguing with his editor at the diner. It was something about "unsubstantiated claims" and "potential legal issues." Wolfram sat three booths away, pretending to read a book but watching the whole scene unfold with those cold eyes of his.

When Chenowith stormed out, I followed him to a bar where he drank himself into a stupor. The man poured out his troubles to anyone who would listen, how his big break had been snatched away, how his girlfriend Margaret was suddenly "too busy" to see him, how his rent was due and his bank account empty.

And yet, when Wolfram appeared at the bar around midnight, Chenowith practically fell over himself to speak with him. The vampire slid an envelope across the table. I suspect it was money, from the way Chenowith's eyes widened, and just like that, all was forgiven. The writer left with Wolfram, notebook already out, hanging on the monster's every word.

The money must be too good for Chenowith to walk away. Or perhaps Wolfram has him under some kind of thrall. Either way, the poor bastard is caught in a web he doesn't even see.

Night 9: I've confirmed my theory. Wolfram doesn't just feed on blood; he feeds on suffering. I watched him orchestrate a public humiliation for Chenowith today at the town's only upscale restaurant. Wolfram arrived with Margaret on his arm, dressed to the nines, and requested a table next to where Chenowith was dining with his editor, attempting to salvage his career.

The look on Chenowith's face was worth a thousand words. Betrayal, jealousy, rage; all these emotions played across his features while Wolfram savored them like fine wine. The vampire actually closed his eyes for a moment, inhaling deeply as if breathing in Chenowith's pain.

Yet tomorrow, I know Chenowith will be back at Wolfram's side, scribbling notes for this "biography" that will likely never see publication. The pattern is clear now. Wolfram builds him up, tears him down, then offers just enough hope to keep him coming back. It's a cruel game, but an effective feeding strategy.

I need to find a way to approach Chenowith alone. If I can make him understand what Wolfram truly is, perhaps he can help me. The Rose and Raven Society would be interested in his notes, at the very least.

For now, I'll continue my surveillance. Wolfram may think he's the hunter here, but he doesn't realize he's being hunted as well. I need to get permission from the field agents of the

Rose and Raven to off this bastard vampire before he kills the poor guy. I will follow him again in the night to see if he feeds on blood. He doesn't seem to need it anywhere near what an average vampire does, adding to my suspicions that he is also a psychic vampire.

Chapter 7
The Hunt

From a Vampire's Perspective

The hunt is both an art and a necessity, a dance on the edge of life and death. For vampires, it is the cornerstone of our existence, the act that sustains us and reminds us of what we have become. To hunt is to embrace our nature, to feel the pulse of life in another being, and to claim a fragment of it for ourselves. Yet, it is not without its perils, nor without its moral weight. It is understandable how some vampires fall to the intoxicating effects of the hunt and descend into murderous intent.

The Thrill of the Hunt

There is no sensation in the world quite like the hunt. It begins with the search, a predator moving unseen among the unsuspecting. The streets at night become a tapestry of possibilities, crowded bars, dimly lit alleys, or the quiet solitude of a park bench. Every human pulse is a drumbeat, every movement a clue. The thrill is in the chase, the anticipation of choosing the right prey, the perfect moment to strike.

I remember one hunt vividly. It was a warm summer night in the early nineteen hundreds, the city alive with laughter and music. I had been watching a young woman in a crowded club, her energy vibrant, her blood singing to me even from across the room. She danced as though the world around her didn't exist, her joy intoxicating. I followed her when she left, keeping my distance, my senses tuned to her every move.

When the moment came, I moved swiftly, guiding her into the shadows with a soft word and a subtle touch. She looked at me with wide, trusting eyes, and for a brief moment, I hesitated. But the hunger was too strong. My fangs pierced her neck, and her warm blood flowed into me, filling the void within. It was ecstasy, a rush of life that no mortal could ever understand. I left her dazed but unharmed, her memory of the encounter already slipping away. There is a sense of loss and an underlying feeling of taint, but I take comfort in the fact I leave my prey unscathed and alive.

The Danger of the Hunt

The hunt is not without its risks. Humans are not as helpless as they seem, and the modern world is fraught with dangers for creatures like me. Surveillance cameras, cell phones, and forensic technology make it increasingly difficult to remain unseen. A careless vampire can easily expose themselves, and the consequences of such a mistake are severe—not just for the individual, but for our entire kind.

There are also the hunters, humans who know of our existence, despite our best efforts to stay hidden, who dedicate their lives to destroying us. They are rare but relentless, and the slightest misstep can draw their attention. I have encountered them only once, and it was enough to teach me caution. The memory of their silver blades and holy symbols still haunts me.

The Ethics of Feeding

For all its exhilaration, the hunt carries a heavy moral burden. Feeding on humans is not something I take lightly. Each time I sink my fangs into a neck, I am acutely aware of the life I am intruding upon. Humans are not mere cattle; they are thinking, feeling beings. To take something, no matter how small, away from them without consent feels like a violation, even if I leave them alive and unharmed.

Some vampires justify their actions by claiming that humans are inferior, that our needs outweigh theirs. I cannot agree. I see the act of feeding as a necessary evil, one that must be approached with care and respect. This is why I never kill when I feed. I take only what I need and ensure that my prey is left with no memory of the encounter. It is the least I can do to preserve their dignity and my own.

There are alternatives, of course. Some vampires subsist on animal blood or donations from willing humans. I have tried both, but neither satisfies the hunger in the same way. Animal blood is thin and lifeless, and while donors are a kinder option, they are rare and often unreliable. The truth is, there is no perfect solution. To be a vampire is to live with the knowledge that your survival comes at a cost.

Reflections on the Hunt

The hunt is a paradox of both pleasure and guilt, a reminder of our power and our dependence. It is what defines us as vampires, separating us from the humans we once were. And yet, it is also what binds us to them. We are predators, but we are also part of the same fragile web of life.

I often wonder if there will ever come a time when we no longer need to hunt, when science or magic might free us from the cycle of hunger and feeding. Until then, I will continue to walk the line between predator and protector, striving to balance my nature with my conscience. For in the end, the hunt is not just about survival, it is about understanding who we are and what we are willing to become.

Chapter 8
From My Own Writings
My First Vampire Hunter Encounter

After re-reading the previous entry to this journal over the hunt, I realized that at the time of the writing I had only had one encounter with vampire hunters. My how things have changed. It seemed like such a rare occurrence back then. I have too many encounters with them now under my belt to count. Still that first time will never leave me. I am going to reconstruct the encounter. The entry and journal of the account is now lost but not forgotten. I remember it well enough to write it here:

It was in the early nineteen hundreds. I had boarded a train to return home. I had recently fed and was in good spirits and ready for the train ride.

The first hunter who tracked me called himself John Desmond. A curious man with a weathered face and hands calloused from years of manual labor. He disguised himself as an elderly gentleman, but I spotted him immediately. The scent of silver nitrate solution on his skin gave him away. Silver Nitrate is a common preparation among hunters who lack the funds for pure silver weapons.

He boarded the same train as me, taking the berth next to mine. Amateur move. True professionals maintain distance. Throughout that first night, I heard him shifting in his bunk, the scratch of pencil on paper as he documented my movements.

I played along, pretending ignorance. For three days, we traveled across the countryside, locked in our silent game. He followed me to the dining car where I pushed food around my plate. He lingered outside the library car while I read. Always watching, always scribbling in that little notebook of his.

On the fourth night, I decided to end our charade. I left my compartment after midnight, making enough noise to wake him. As expected, he followed me to the observation car, empty at that late hour.

"Beautiful night," I said without turning around. "Don't you think, Mr. Desmond?"

The sharp intake of breath behind me was satisfying. "How do you know my name?"

I turned to face him. "The same way I know you're carrying a wooden stake in your left boot and holy water in that flask. The same way I know the Rose and Raven Society sent you."

His hand moved toward his coat pocket. I was beside him before he could blink.

"I wouldn't," I whispered. "We're alone here, and I've fed recently."

Fear flashed across his face, quickly replaced by determination. "You're a monster. I've read your file."

"My file?" I laughed. "How flattering. What does it say?"

"That you've killed dozens. That you toy with your victims before feeding."

I stepped back, genuinely surprised. "Is that what they told you? Interesting. Someone has confused me with another of my kind."

"All vampires are killers," he spat.

"Like all humans are saints?" I gestured to the empty seat across from me. "Sit. If you wanted me dead, you'd have tried already."

Reluctantly, he sat. For the next hour, we talked. I explained my philosophy on feeding without killing. He listened with skepticism but didn't reach for his weapons again.

"Why should I believe you?" he finally asked.

"You shouldn't. Trust nothing from a vampire's mouth. But observe my actions. I've known you were hunting me since you boarded. If I were the monster in your file, why are you still breathing?"

Dawn approached. I stood to leave. "Follow me if you must, Mr. Desmond. But perhaps consider that your society doesn't know everything about my kind."

I left him there, contemplating. For the remainder of our journey, he watched me from a distance, but the hostility in his gaze had diminished.

When we reached our destination, I lost him in the crowd deliberately. A small mercy. Hunters rarely retire instead they either succeed or die trying. I wanted neither fate for him.

Three months later, I read about his death in a newspaper. Found in an alley with his throat torn out, his weapons untouched. The article mentioned his connection to a "secretive research organization."

I didn't kill John Desmond. I suspect he encountered another vampire, one who matched the description in my "file." Perhaps he hesitated, remembering our conversation. Perhaps that hesitation cost him his life.

I sometimes wonder if I should have killed him that night on the train. It might have been kinder than leaving him to face a true monster unprepared. But I've never taken a human life, and I wasn't about to start with someone who was, in his misguided way, trying to protect others.

The Rose and Raven Society sent more hunters after that. Better trained. More cautious. None ever got as close as John Desmond.

Chapter 9
The Hunter Being Hunted

A Vampire's Guide to Survival: The Threat of Vampire Hunter

The history of vampire hunting is as old as the existence of vampires themselves. For as long as we have walked the earth, there have been those who have sought to destroy us. These hunters, armed with knowledge passed down through generations, are both our greatest threat and our greatest fascination. They are the reason we remain hidden, the reason we tread carefully in the shadows.

The History of Vampire Hunting

The earliest accounts of vampire hunters date back to the Dark Ages, when superstition ruled, and humanity feared the night. Back then, hunting was crude and often indiscriminate. Villages would burn suspected vampires at the stake or drive stakes into the hearts of corpses thought to be rising from the grave. These methods were as likely to kill innocents as they were to harm us, but they marked the beginning of an enduring battle.

As time passed, vampire hunters became more organized and sophisticated. Secret societies formed, their members dedicated to studying our weaknesses and perfecting their methods. The greatest and most secretive among them is the Rose and Raven Society. Just writing the name of the organization feels me with dread. The Church also played a significant role in this evolution, equipping hunters with holy relics, silver weapons, and sacred texts that detailed our vulnerabilities. By the Renaissance, hunters had become a formidable force, capable of identifying and eliminating vampires with chilling efficiency.

Today, vampire hunting has entered a new era. Modern hunters use technology to track us, employing thermal imaging, DNA testing, and advanced weaponry. They are no longer driven solely by superstition or religion; many are scientists, mercenaries, or individuals with personal vendettas. They are relentless, and their methods are more precise than ever.

Encounters with Vampire Hunters

Since beginning this journal, I have faced hunters on several occasions, and each encounter has left its mark. However, my first and most harrowing memory stands out above the rest, a night that tested my wits and my will to survive.

It began in a quiet town where I had been living for several months. I had been careful, feeding sparingly and leaving no trace of my presence. But somehow, I had been discovered. Perhaps it was a careless slip, or perhaps the hunters were simply more skilled than I had anticipated. Either way, they came for me.

The first sign was the scent of silver in the air, a metallic tang that burned my senses. Then came the sound of footsteps, deliberate and measured. They were closing in. I fled, darting through the narrow streets, my heightened senses scanning for an escape route. They were from the Rose and Raven, and they were prepared, blocking every exit with traps and weapons designed to weaken me.

In the end, it was not strength that saved me but cunning. I lured them into an abandoned building, using the shadows to my advantage. One by one, I disabled them, careful not to kill. It would have been easy to end their lives, but I knew that doing so would only attract more hunters. Instead, I left them unconscious, their weapons destroyed and then I disappeared into the night.

Tips for Evading Vampire Hunters

Surviving in a world where hunters exist requires more than just strength and speed. It demands strategy, discipline, and a deep understanding of human behavior. Here are some of the lessons I have learned:

Blend In: The most effective way to avoid hunters is to appear as human as possible. Dress inconspicuously, maintain a modest lifestyle, and avoid drawing attention to yourself. The more ordinary you seem, the less likely you are to be noticed.

Control Your Hunger: Overfeeding or leaving a trail of victims is a surefire way to attract hunters. Take only what you need and ensure that your prey is left unharmed and unaware of what has happened.

Study Your Enemy: Knowledge is power. Learn everything you can about hunters—their tactics, their tools, and their weaknesses. Anticipate their moves and stay one step ahead.

Avoid Patterns: Hunters are skilled at detecting routines. Change your feeding grounds, your routes, and your habits frequently. Never stay in one place for too long.

Use Decoys: If you suspect you are being followed, create false trails to mislead your pursuers. Leave behind items that suggest you have fled in one direction while you escape in another.

Allies Are Key: Never underestimate the value of a trusted ally. Whether it's another vampire or a human friend, having someone to watch your back can mean the difference between survival and capture.

The Eternal Dance

The relationship between vampires and hunters is a paradox. They are our greatest threat, yet they are also a reminder of our power. Without hunters, we might grow careless, arrogant. Their existence keeps us sharp, forcing us to adapt and evolve.

I do not hate them, these hunters who dedicate their lives to destroying mine. I understand them. They see us as monsters, as predators who prey on the innocent. In their place, I might feel the same. But I also know that we are more than the sum of our instincts. We are creatures of the night, yes, but we are also beings of thought, emotion, and restraint.

The hunt continues, an eternal dance between predator and prey, hunter and hunted. And as long as I walk on this earth, I will do whatever it takes to survive. For in the end, survival is the truest expression of what it means to be alive, even for those of us who are no longer living.

Chapter 10
From the Writings of
Denholm Smith
Rose and Raven Vampire Hunter Entry IV

We had him cornered. My silver medallion glowed red with the anticipation of me staking the bastard once and for all. Vampires are the truest predator, but man is the deadliest. Living beings have the advantage of sharp wits and quick minds. Vampire wits are unnatural and of the devil, no match for God's true creatures. I lost him for a time, which is why my entries skip days. I found him on my 14th day of being assigned to him.

Night 14: I've lost track of Wolfram for three days. After our last encounter at the café, he vanished completely. There was no trace at the hotel, the library, or any of his usual haunts. I feared he'd fled town, but today I spotted him again, looking remarkably well-fed and composed. Too composed.

He was outside the newspaper office, deep in conversation with a tall man I hadn't seen before. Not Chenowith, who was nowhere to be found. This newcomer carried himself with confidence. He wore an expensive suit, leather portfolio, and seemed to have a firm handshake. I overheard the name "Morrison" when they parted ways.

Later, I followed Morrison to the Grand Hotel. The desk clerk called him "Mr. Morrison" with the deference reserved for important guests. A writer, perhaps? Or something else entirely?

My suspicions were confirmed when I saw Wolfram's expression as he watched Morrison leave. There was calculation in those eyes, and something darker. The same look he had before he began systematically destroying Chenowith's life.

Speaking of Chenowith, he's been absent for two days now. His editor at the paper seemed concerned, mentioned something about missed deadlines. I need to find him before Wolfram does whatever he's planning.

Night 15: Chenowith is alive, but barely holding it together. I found him at a rundown motel on the edge of town, room paid through the week. He jumped when I knocked, peered through the curtains before opening the door a crack.

"Who sent you?" His eyes were bloodshot, his clothes rumpled.

I convinced him I was a colleague investigating Wolfram for a magazine piece. He let me in, then checked the parking lot twice before locking the door.

"He's going to kill me," Chenowith whispered, hands shaking as he poured himself a drink. "I've seen what he is."

Turns out Chenowith accidentally discovered pages from Wolfram's personal journal while transcribing their interviews. The vampire had stepped out, and curiosity got the better of him. What he read terrified him enough to run.

"And now there's this Morrison guy," he said, slumping onto the bed. "Taking my place. Same pattern. Wolfram finds a writer, promises exclusive access, then—" He made a slashing motion across his throat.

I pressed for details about Morrison. First name unknown, but apparently he's from some prestigious publishing house in New York. Wolfram approached him directly, claiming dissatisfaction with Chenowith's work.

"He'll do to Morrison what he did to me," Chenowith muttered. "Build him up, tear him down. But Morrison won't run. He'll stay until it's too late."

I left Chenowith with strict instructions to remain hidden and contact no one. Tomorrow I'll research this Morrison character. If he's Wolfram's next victim, he deserves warning whether he'll believe me or not.

Night 16: Morrison's first name is James. James Morrison, senior editor at Blackwood Publishing, specializing in biographies of "extraordinary individuals." I found his credentials impressive enough to warrant a meeting.

We met at a café far from Wolfram's usual haunts. Morrison was skeptical at first, another writer interested in his subject, but professional curiosity won out.

"Wolfram is fascinating," he said, stirring his coffee. "His knowledge of historical events is uncanny. Almost as if he'd witnessed them firsthand."

I watched his face carefully as I asked about Chenowith. A flicker of discomfort crossed his features.

"Unfortunate situation. Wolfram said the man became obsessed, started fabricating stories. Mental health issues, apparently."

"And you believe that?"

Morrison shrugged. "Creative types can be unstable. Besides, Wolfram has been nothing but forthcoming with me. We've already signed an exclusive contract."

I tried a different approach, asking about Wolfram's habits like his avoidance of daylight, his untouched meals, his cold touch. Morrison dismissed each observation with rational explanations: photosensitivity, dietary restrictions, poor circulation.

"You sound defensive," I noted. "Almost protective."

"I protect my investments," he replied coolly. "This biography will make my career."

As we parted ways, I slipped my card into his pocket. "When you start noticing the inconsistencies, call me."

Morrison's smile was insincere, I could tell. "I appreciate your concern, Mr. Smith. But I assure you, I know exactly what I'm doing."

I'm not convinced. The pattern is clear. Wolfram is setting Morrison up just as he did Chenowith. But why? What does he gain from this elaborate game? If he simply wanted to feed, there are easier targets.

No, this is something else. Something to do with these biographies that never see publication. I need to find Wolfram's previous writers, if any survived. The Rose and Raven Society archives might have records.

Meanwhile, I'll keep watch over both Chenowith and Morrison. Wolfram won't claim another victim on my watch.

Chapter II
Vampires Hunting Humans

The Peril of the Hunt: When Vampires Hunt Humans

Hunting humans is the most dangerous and controversial act among vampires. It is not merely a question of survival but a delicate balancing act between our instincts and the unyielding need to remain hidden. The dangers are manifold, not just for the prey but for the predator as well. Yet, despite the risks, some vampires still choose to hunt recklessly, driven by desperation, arrogance, or sheer thrill-seeking.

The Dangers of Hunting Humans

Hunting humans carries inherent risks that extend far beyond the act itself. The modern world is not kind to secrets. Surveillance cameras, social media, and forensic technology have made it increasingly difficult to cover our tracks. A single mistake—a body left behind, a witness who remembers too much—can unravel the veil of secrecy that protects us.

But the greatest danger lies in the humans themselves. They are not as weak as they seem. Some are armed, trained, or simply unpredictable in their will to survive. I have seen vampires brought low by a well-placed silver blade or a bullet laced with ultraviolet compounds. Even the most experienced hunter can fall victim to a moment of carelessness.

Then there are the psychological dangers. To hunt a human is to confront your own predatory nature. For some, this is exhilarating. For others, it is a reminder of what we have lost—the humanity that slips further away with each feeding. The act of taking blood, of feeling their life force flow into you, is both intimate and violent. It is a connection unlike any other, but it is also a stark reminder of the divide between what we are and what they are.

The Effects of a Vampire's Bite

Being bitten by a vampire is not the romanticized experience portrayed in human fiction. It is a profound violation, both physical and psychological. The bite itself is sharp, a sudden burst of pain followed by a numbing euphoria. This is not an accident; our venom contains compounds that dull the senses and cloud the mind, making it easier for us to feed without resistance.

But the effects linger. Physically, the victim may experience fatigue, dizziness, and anemia. The wound heals quickly, thanks to the properties of our saliva, but it leaves a faint scar—a mark that some humans wear with pride and others with shame.

Psychologically, the experience is more complex. Some humans report vivid dreams or feelings of inexplicable connection to the vampire who bit them. Others are left with a gnawing sense of fear or paranoia, as though they can still feel our presence long after we are gone. The most dangerous effect, however, is the compulsion. If the vampire chooses, they can implant a subtle suggestion, bending the victim's will to their own. This power is rarely used, as it risks drawing unwanted attention, but it is a reminder of the delicate balance we must maintain.

Stories of Reckless Hunters

I once knew a vampire named Rossini, a bold and reckless hunter who reveled in the thrill of the chase. He saw humans not as individuals but as sport, their lives inconsequential compared to his hunger. Rossini hunted openly, leaving a trail of bodies that could not be ignored.

The Elders warned him, but he did not listen. "Humans are weak," he said, dismissing their concerns. "They will never catch me."

He was wrong.

It was one of the agents of the Rose and Raven Society, a man posing as a small-town sheriff, who brought him down, armed with nothing but determination and a makeshift stake. Rossini underestimated his prey, and in his arrogance, he made a fatal mistake. The sheriff's actions drew the attention of his fellow vampire hunters, and soon the entire brethren was forced to relocate, abandoning centuries of carefully built lives to escape the fallout.

The consequences of Rossini's actions were a harsh reminder of the price of carelessness. He was not mourned.

The Delicate Balance

To hunt humans is to walk a razor's edge. We are predators, but we are also sentient beings capable of choice. The act of feeding is not inherently evil, but the way it is done can define us. Some vampires, like Rossini, see humans as nothing more than prey. Others, like myself, approach the hunt with caution and respect, taking only what is necessary and leaving no trace.

I have fed on humans, but I have never killed. Each time, I am careful to erase the memory of the encounter, to ensure that they wake with no more than a faint sense of unease and a fleeting mark on their skin. It is not a perfect solution, but it is the best I can do to reconcile my nature with my conscience.

The hunt is dangerous, yes, but it is also inevitable. It is the price we pay for our immortality, the shadow that follows us through eternity. To be a vampire is to live with this paradox, to embrace the darkness within while striving to keep it from consuming us entirely. For in the end, it is not the hunt that defines us, but the choices we make along the way.

I have some more entries from another vampire hunter. I collect vampire hunter memorabilia so again, just for the sake of clarity, I did nothing to these people personally. I find bits and pieces of their notes in various places and snatch them up either by purchasing them or finding their work lying about.

Chapter 12
From the Report of Sheriff Jose Jimenez
Entry 6

I have spotted the vampire, but I am unprepared for him. I have my sheriff department issued gun and club, but neither will do me much good. The bullets are not silver, and the club is polished and painted. If I could break it somehow into a dagger of sharp wood, it might be handy but that's nearly impossible. There has to be a way for me to subdue him with what I have available to me. I found my good hunting knife. There are some trees nearby. Perhaps if I were to cut one of the skinnier branches with the knife I could fashion a sharp stick strong enough to do the trick. This vampire has been careless and led me right to him, but he's no pushover. I'll have to use his momentum against him.

The deed is done. I think he broke my arm, but I managed to stick him in the chest with my sharpened elm branch. He howled and screamed, and I could tell he couldn't believe I got the best of him. He killed no less than five in this medium sized county and I for one am glad to have dispatched him. The R&R society did send me backup, but they arrived after I had already got the bastard. The agent I talked to tonight said the society will promote me into their ranks after this one. I don't care about that. I am just glad another one of those terrible monsters is dealt with and will not kill again.

I am not a full member of the R&R society, but I have been offered a training position. I am following a man named Henry Stoggins into the field tonight. He is looking into a vampire named Sabastian Wolfram. I am shadowing him in the trip.

October 6, 1963: The night air bit into my skin as I followed Henry through the darkened streets. His confident stride betrayed years of experience hunting these creatures. My own steps felt clumsy in comparison, but I kept pace, my hand never far from my modified service revolver loaded with silver bullets - courtesy of the Rose and Raven Society.

"Stay sharp, Jose," Henry whispered, his breath visible in the cold. "Wolfram's different from your average bloodsucker. He's smart, calculated."

We tracked Wolfram to an abandoned theater on the outskirts of town. The building's facade loomed above us, its windows like dead eyes staring down at potential prey. Henry motioned for me to circle around back while he took the front entrance.

"Remember your training," he said, checking his weapons one last time. "If you see him, don't engage. Signal me."

I nodded, throat dry. The back alley reeked of rotting garbage and something metallic - blood. Fresh blood. My fingers trembled as I drew my gun, the silver cross around my neck suddenly feeling too light for comfort.

A crash echoed from inside. Then Henry's voice: "Jose! He's here!"

I burst through the back door, gun raised. The theater's interior was a maze of torn curtains and broken seats. It was dark and shadows danced across the walls, playing tricks with my vision. Henry's flashlight beam cut through the darkness ahead.

"Up there!" Henry shouted, pointing to the balcony.

A figure moved with impossible speed, more shadow than substance. Henry fired twice, the gunshots deafening in the enclosed space. The figure laughed - a sound that froze my blood.

"Henry Stoggins," a voice purred from the darkness. "The Society sends its best."

I crept forward, trying to get a better angle. Henry backed toward the stage, his experienced eyes scanning every corner.

"Show yourself, Wolfram!"

Another laugh, closer this time. "Why rush? The night is young."

The attack came from above. One moment Henry stood ready, the next he was airborne, thrown across the theater like a ragdoll. His body hit the stage with a sickening crack.

"Henry!" I screamed, firing blindly toward the movement.

The vampire, Wolfram, materialized beside me, knocking the gun from my hand. His face was young, but his eyes held centuries of malice. He grabbed my throat, lifting me off my feet.

"The Society recruits children now?" His grip tightened. "How disappointing."

Henry's voice, weak but determined, cut through my panic: "Run, Jose!"

Wolfram turned, giving me the opening I needed. I drove my silver cross into his arm. He hissed, dropping me. I scrambled for my gun, but a scream stopped me cold.

Henry hung suspended in Wolfram's grasp, blood trickling from his mouth. "I said run!" he gasped.

I hesitated, torn between duty and survival. Henry's eyes met mine one last time before Wolfram's hands twisted. The crack of breaking bone echoed through the theater.

My legs carried me through the back door, into the alley, my lungs burning. Behind me, Wolfram's laughter followed like a curse. I ran until my legs gave out, collapsing in a different alley blocks away.

Henry was dead. The Society's best hunter, killed in seconds. And I had run like a coward.

I pulled out my notebook with shaking hands, needing to record what happened while it was fresh. The Society needed to know. Everyone needed to know what we were really up against.

Chapter 13
The Curse of Becoming a Vampire

The Vampire's Curse: The Cost of Immortality: Becoming a Vampire

The choice to become a vampire—or the lack of choice, as is often the case—is not one to be taken lightly. It is a transformation that changes every aspect of who you are, reshaping your body, mind, and very existence. While the allure of immortality is undeniable, the consequences are profound and often devastating. I know this because I've lived it, and I've seen others struggle with the weight of their new lives.

The Physical Changes

The first thing you notice after becoming a vampire is the body's transformation. It begins almost immediately, a surge of power and vitality that courses through every vein. Your senses sharpen to an almost unbearable degree. Colors are more vivid, sounds are more distinct, and every scent carries a complexity you have never imagined. The human world becomes overwhelming in its detail, and it takes time to learn how to filter the constant influx of information.

Your strength and speed increase exponentially. I once crushed a steel pipe in my hand without realizing my own power. It is exhilarating, but it also requires discipline. Without control, even a simple handshake can turn into a display of monstrous force.

The most striking change, however, is the hunger. It begins as a dull ache, but it grows quickly into a gnawing, insatiable need. Your body craves blood, not just as sustenance but as a source of life itself. It is a hunger that never truly goes away, always lingering in the back of your mind, a constant ache and a constant reminder of what you have become.

The Psychological Changes

The psychological effects of becoming a vampire are even more profound. You are no longer human, and that realization is both liberating and isolating. The people you once loved become strangers, their warmth and vitality a painful reminder of what you have lost. Time itself becomes a burden. Days turn into years, and years into centuries, leaving you adrift in a world that moves on without you.

Many new vampires struggle with their identity. Am I still the person I was before? Or am I something entirely new? The answer is never simple. The memories of your human life remain, but they feel distant, like echoes of a dream. You are both yourself and a stranger, a paradox that can drive some to madness, and it does.

Stories of the Turned

I remember a young man named Marcus, one of the first people I turned. He had been dying of an illness, his body wasting away before my eyes. In a moment of weakness, I offered him a second chance to live. He accepted, and I performed the ritual that would make him one of us.

At first, Marcus was ecstatic. His body healed, his strength returned, and he reveled in the power of his new existence. But the joy was short-lived. He struggled with the hunger, the need for blood consuming his thoughts. He refused to feed for weeks, clinging on to his humanity, but it only made him weaker and more desperate. When he finally gave in, the act shattered him. He wept for hours afterward, unable to reconcile the predator he had become with the man he once was.

Then there was Eliza, a woman who had been turned against her will. She had been attacked by a rogue vampire, left to die in an alley. I found her and helped her through the transition, but much like me, she never forgave the one who had cursed her. Eliza was consumed by rage, and it drove her to hunt the vampire who had turned her. When she finally found him, she killed him without hesitation. But the act did not bring her peace. Instead, it left her hollow, her vengeance a bitter reminder of what she had lost. Her ordeal made me think twice about my own situation.

The Consequences of Immortality

Becoming a vampire is not just a change; it is a severance. You are cut off from the life you once knew, from the people you once loved. You gain immortality, but you lose the ability to connect with the mortal world. Relationships become fleeting, and the passage of time turns even the deepest bonds into distant memories.

There is also the moral weight of your existence. To survive, you must feed, and to feed, you must take from others. Some vampires embrace this, reveling in their predatory nature. Others, like myself, struggle with the ethical implications. I know I have said this before, but I really want to reiterate that I take only what I need, leaving my prey alive and unharmed, even if it sometimes, or always, feels like a violation.

Finding a Way Forward

Despite the challenges, there is a way forward. Becoming a vampire is not the end; it is a new beginning. It is a chance to see the world in ways you have never imagined, to experience life from a perspective that few can understand. But it is also a test—a test of your will, your morality, and your capacity to endure.

I have seen others fail this test, consumed by their hunger or their despair. But I have also seen those who thrive, who find purpose and meaning in their new existence. For me, the key is balance. I embrace what I have become, but I do not let it define me. I am a vampire, yes, but I am also more than that. I am still me, in whatever form that takes.

Chapter 14
From the Writings of Elizabeth Blount
Fledgling Vampire Entry 7

I saw him tonight. He was walking along River Street. I know what he wants. He is looking for his next victim. He has a routine. He hunts in the same way each and every time I have found him. He will not escape me this night. I will stay in the shadows and mask myself from him. I have learned to separate myself from his heightened senses. He will not detect me this time. I will kill him. It might not return me to what I once was, but I know it will give me some peace, some closure. In my research, I have found that he must not be that old of a vampire because he is clumsy and not very cunning. I almost think it was a fluke he found me and turned me. I am not even sure he meant to turn me.

He took a young woman from the front of a coffee shop and dragged her into the alley. She was not screaming and kicking the way I did when he took me. He has gotten better at using his charm and mesmerism. I noticed he also did a preliminary bite, which explains why the girl is compliant. She has been injected with vampire blood and rendered docile. He has her against the wall. I will sneak up behind him.

He's dead! I sneaked up on him and took him from behind, slicing his throat with my knife. After his initial shock, I was satisfied to see his eyes go wide with recognition when his dull eyes focused on my face. I yelled Fuck you bastard and shoved my stake through his heart. He convulsed as I accidentally shoved the stake all the way through him. I retrieved the stake and stabbed him with it again and again, before feeding on his victim myself. I made sure her memory was altered before I returned her to the coffee shop.

It's funny, I thought I would find comfort in my maker's death, but I have not. I feel empty now, like I killed my father, which makes no sense to me. I stopped by Sabastian's house and told him what I had done. He told me several times he wanted to do the same with his maker and I wanted to fill him in on what I have done. He was understanding and kind as normal, but I could see in his eyes, he was judging me.

Chapter 15
Vampire Relationships

Eternal Love: The Complexities of Vampire Relationships

Romance among vampires is as timeless as our existence and as complicated as the eternity we share. We may no longer be human, but our hearts are still capable of love—perhaps even more deeply than before. Yet, the challenges of sustaining a relationship as immortals are unique, fraught with complexities that only those who live forever can understand.

The Nature of Vampire Love

When two vampires fall in love, it is an all-consuming bond. Our heightened senses and emotions make every connection more intense. Love is sharper, deeper, and more enduring. But with eternity stretching before us, even the strongest relationships can face trials that would shatter a mortal union.

One of the greatest challenges is time. For humans, love is fleeting, a bright flame that burns against the inevitability of mortality. For us, there is no such urgency. This can be both a blessing and a curse. Without the pressure of time, relationships can evolve slowly, unfolding over decades or even centuries. But eternity also has a way of amplifying flaws and magnifying doubts. A small irritation can grow into an insurmountable chasm when you have centuries to dwell on it.

Another challenge is the hunger. Feeding is an intimate act, and jealousy can arise when one partner feeds on others. While most vampire couples establish rules or boundaries around feeding, these agreements are not always easy to uphold. The line between necessity and desire can blur, leading to misunderstandings and conflicts.

Stories of Vampire Couples

I once knew a pair of vampires, Orion [pronounced or-e-un] and Iris, whose love story was as passionate as it was tragic. They met in the late 18th century, drawn to each other by a shared love of art and philosophy. For decades, they were inseparable, their bond unshakable. But over time, cracks began to form. Orion's hunger for adventure clashed with Iris's desire for stability. He wanted to explore the world, while she preferred the quiet solitude of their home.

Their relationship unraveled slowly, each argument chipping away at their connection. The final blow came when Orion fed on a mortal without consulting Iris, breaking an unspoken agreement between them. Though he claimed it was an act of necessity, she saw it as a betrayal. They parted ways, their love unable to withstand the weight of eternity.

On the other hand, I have seen vampire couples thrive. Take Lunare and Selene, who have been together for nearly three centuries. Their secret lies in their shared purpose. They work together to protect younger vampires, offering guidance and support to those struggling with their new existence. This shared mission gives their relationship meaning, binding them together in a way that transcends personal differences.

Advice for Vampire Relationships

For those of us who seek to navigate the complexities of love as immortals, there are lessons to be learned:

Communicate Openly: Eternity is too long to harbor secrets or resentments. Be honest about your needs, fears, and desires. Silence can be more damaging than any argument.

Respect Boundaries: Feeding habits are a common source of conflict among vampire couples. Establish clear boundaries and respect them. If you decide to feed outside the relationship, ensure it is done with transparency and consent.

Embrace Change: Even as immortals, we are not immune to change. Over centuries, your partner will evolve, as will you.

Accept these changes and adapt together, rather than clinging to the past.

Find a Shared Purpose: A relationship built solely on passion can fade over time. Find something that unites you beyond love, a mission, a project, or a shared interest. This will give your bond a foundation that can withstand the trials of eternity.

Give Each Other Space: Eternity can be suffocating if you spend every moment together. Allow each other the freedom to pursue individual interests and experiences. Absence, even brief, can make the heart grow fonder.

Remember The Immortal Dance

Love among vampires is not so different from love among humans. It is a dance of connection and compromise, passion and patience. But the stakes are higher, the emotions more intense, and the consequences more enduring. To love as a vampire is to embrace vulnerability in the face of immortality, to risk pain for the chance at a bond that can last forever.

I have loved and lost, and I have loved and endured. Each relationship has taught me something new about myself and about what it means to share eternity with another. For those of us who walk the night, love is both a refuge and a challenge, a reminder that even in the darkness, there is light. And perhaps that is what makes it worth pursuing, again and again, across the endless stretch of time.

Chapter 16
From the Writings of Lunare and Selene
Vampire Lovers Entry 8

I am working with a young vampire brought to me by Sabastian Wolfram whom we often affectionately call Wolfy. The subject is a young female vampire with whom I believe Wolfy is interesting in conducting a relationship. Wolfy appears to be around thirty years of age, but I have known him personally for centuries. This young vampire is only twenty-five years old in her human life and mere months in her reborn, vampiric life.

One might think it strange that such an age difference is not condemned by us. However, despite the centuries long age differences, in appearance, they are within a few years of one another. Who is to say one soul is not centuries older than the other even in the years of humans? I have heard of children being called 'old souls' and the like. If the soul is immortal, then age is not nearly as important as the appearance of age.

Obviously, one would not get romantically involved with anyone before the age of puberty, but once puberty is completed, who knows the true age of the soul and who cares, really. I will allow this relationship as long as both parties are willing. I see nothing wrong with it. True age and the appearance of age is not a concern.

Chapter 17
Vampire Communities

The Hidden World of Vampire Communities

Vampires are real, and we are not solitary creatures. While the popular image of the lone predator stalking the night has some truth to it, the reality is far richer and more complex. Across the globe, vampire communities thrive in the shadows, each with its own customs, hierarchies, and cultural nuances. These communities are as diverse as the humans they live among, shaped by geography, history, and the unique challenges of our existence.

The Variety of Vampire Communities

Vampire communities can be broadly divided into brethrens, clans, and solitary networks. Brethrens are tightly knit groups, often bound by blood ties or shared origins. They are hierarchical, with a leader—often the oldest or most powerful vampire—at the top. Brethrens are common in regions where vampires face significant external threats, such as vampire hunters or rival factions, as unity is essential for survival.

Clans are larger and less rigid, often encompassing multiple brethrens or independent vampires who share a common ancestry or philosophy. Clans are more prevalent in areas with a long history of vampire activity, such as Eastern Europe or parts of Asia. These communities often have elaborate traditions, passed down through generations.

Solitary networks are loose affiliations of vampires who prefer independence but maintain connections for mutual aid. These are most common in urban centers, where anonymity is easier to maintain. Vampires in these networks come together only when necessary, such as to address a threat or exchange information.

Cultural Differences Between Communities

The customs and beliefs of vampire communities vary widely depending on their location and history. In Eastern Europe, for instance, clans often hold elaborate gatherings known as Blood Feasts, where vampires share stories, settle disputes, and honor their ancestors. These events are steeped in ritual, with ancient songs and dances that date back centuries.

In contrast, vampire communities in Japan have a more discreet and minimalist approach. Known as the Kage-no-Kai, or

"Shadow Society," these vampires operate with extreme precision, blending seamlessly into human life. Their feeding rituals are highly ceremonial, emphasizing restraint and harmony. They view the act of feeding as a spiritual exchange, a far cry from the more predatory approach of Western vampires.

In South America, vampire communities often draw from indigenous traditions, blending vampiric customs with local folklore. These vampires see themselves as guardians of the land, feeding sparingly and protecting the balance of nature. They hold nocturnal ceremonies in the rainforest, where they invoke ancient spirits to guide their actions.

Stories of Vampire Communities

One of the most fascinating communities I've encountered was the Night Coven of Paris, a sprawling network of vampires who have thrived in the city for centuries. The Night Coven is a blend of old and new, with ancient vampires presiding over modern factions. They hold court in an abandoned opera house, its grandeur a reminder of their long history. The Night Coven operates like a parliament, with representatives from different brethrens debating laws and policies that govern their kind. It is a delicate balance of power, but it has allowed them to maintain order in a city teeming with vampires.

Another memorable community is the Desert Moon of the Sahara. These vampires are nomadic, moving between oases and ancient ruins. They have adapted to the harsh environment, feeding sparingly and relying on secrecy to survive. Their customs are deeply tied to the desert, with rituals that honor the stars and the endless sands. I spent a month with them once, learning their ways. They taught me the value of patience and the art of survival in the most unforgiving conditions.

Customs and Traditions

Despite their differences, all vampire communities share a few common customs. The most important is the sanctity of secrecy. Every community, regardless of its size or culture, is bound by the unspoken rule to remain hidden from humans. This rule is enforced with unwavering strictness, as exposure threatens not just the individual but the entire community.

Another common tradition is the mentorship of fledglings. When a human is turned into a vampire, it is the responsibility of their sire to teach them the rules and customs of their new life. In some communities, this mentorship lasts for decades, ensuring that the fledgling is fully prepared to navigate the complexities of vampire society.

Reflections on Community

As a vampire, I have been part of many communities, each offering a unique perspective on what it means to live as one of us. Some have welcomed me with open arms, while others have viewed me with suspicion, wary of outsiders. Yet, in every community, I have found a shared understanding, a recognition, that we are bound by our nature and our need to coexist.

Vampire communities are a testament to our resilience and adaptability. They are places of refuge, centers of culture, and networks of support. They remind us that even in the darkness, we are not alone. For as long as vampires exist, these communities will endure, evolving and thriving in the hidden corners of the world.

Chapter 18
From the Writings of Sabastian Wolfram
The Desert Moon of the Sahara Entry 9

This nomad coven is strange. I can't imagine being a traveler who happens upon them. They seem friendly and welcoming and then in the night you are drained of blood and life force. I have not seen them kill, but I know from talking with some of their elder vampires within the coven that they are not above it if necessary. The desert is unforgiving, and one may think it empty and desolate but that would be untrue.

The desert teems with life not only from animals and plants but with bands of nomadic people. There are no shortage of caravans and large groups milling about the vast waste lands. One has to wonder why. Why do so many call the sands of the desert home when other, more forgiving lands are available? I will stick with this group for a while to see if I can find any answers to that question. They have offered one of their own as a mate, but I have been resisting. Vampire mating is different from humans and not something to get into lightly. I am still hung up on Elizabeth anyway. I wonder where she has gone. I hope her experience as a vampire hunter has taught her how to avoid them. I will continue to evaluate the situation and make a final decision before I depart.

The sun had set over the vast, endless expanse of the desert sands. The Desert Moon coven had tracked this caravan for days, waiting for the perfect moment to strike. As the merchants settled in for the night, huddled around flickering fires, the vampires emerged from the shadows like wraiths.

I followed the coven leader, Azrael, his imposing figure cutting through the darkness with ease. My heart raced not with fear but with anticipation - a mix of curiosity and hunger that surprised even me. When had I last given in so completely to my darker impulses?

The attack was swift and silent. In moments, we overwhelmed their guards and descended upon them like ravenous birds upon carrion. I knelt beside one man, a plump middle-aged merchant clutching his chest in terror.

"P-please," he pleaded through trembling lips.

I ignored his words and gripped his wrists tight against my thigh, sinking my fangs deep into his neck with barely a hesitation.

Someone watched me.

That thought rose above the rush of excitement, but something was stirring inside me - something new.

It started as a tingle at the base of my spine - warmth spreading outward until my body felt filled with light. It wasn't just from the blood.

Comprehension dawned swiftly: I was feeding on more than lifeblood; I was sipping at his fear, drinking down his panic.

Then I shut myself off to that suggestion hastily. Experience told me how wrong that idea sounded - almost worse than actually killing a human while eating him! Playing up words to myself was the correct response so he couldn't lull me into one more awful sin. But the words gave no comfort.

Perhaps I'd been wanting this too hard for too long!

I plugged back into him strongly and lost all concern what I sounded like as he and his agony pumped through me again.

Done! Let him go.

I released him, beyond satisfied at his shrill denial of everything! I felt euphoric, high! This kind of feeding could become habit forming!

Chapter 19
Our Ways: Vampire Abilities

The Powers of the Night: A Vampire's Perspective

To be a vampire is to wield powers that defy human understanding, gifts born of darkness and necessity. These abilities are not merely enhancements of mortal traits but entirely new dimensions of existence. They are as varied as the vampires who possess them, each power shaped by the individual's age, strength, and experience. Yet even these gifts come with their own limitations, for nothing in this world is without balance.

The Powers We Possess

The most universal of our abilities is heightened physicality. Our strength far exceeds that of humans, allowing us to perform feats that seem impossible. I have shattered iron locks with a single hand and leaped over walls that would take mortals hours to scale. Our speed is another hallmark, enabling us to move faster than the eye can follow. This is not merely running quickly—it is as though time itself slows for us, allowing us to act in moments that would otherwise be lost.

Our senses are similarly enhanced. I can hear a whisper through stone walls, see clearly in total darkness, and distinguish individual scents in a crowded room. This sensory acuity is both a gift and a burden, as the world becomes overwhelming in its detail. It takes years to learn how to filter the constant barrage of information.

Beyond these physical traits, some vampires possess more esoteric powers. One of the most common is mesmerism—the ability to influence the minds of others. With a glance or a few words, I can plant suggestions, erase memories, or bend a person's will to my own. This power is subtle, requiring finesse and practice, but it is invaluable for maintaining our secrecy.

Another ability is shadow manipulation. Some vampires can meld with the darkness, becoming nearly invisible in low light. I have used this power to evade pursuers and observe unseen. Older vampires often develop even more extraordinary abilities, such as telekinesis, weather manipulation, or the rare and feared power of pyrokinesis—the ability to summon and control fire.

Strengths and Limitations

While our powers are formidable, they are not without limits. Strength and speed, for example, are tied to our physical condition. If a vampire is weakened from lack of feeding, these abilities diminish significantly. Similarly, mesmerism requires focus and proximity; a distracted mind or a strong-willed target can resist its effects.

Shadow manipulation is effective only in darkness. In brightly lit areas, this ability is useless, forcing us to rely on more conventional means of concealment. Other powers, such as telekinesis or pyrokinesis, drain energy quickly, leaving the vampire vulnerable if overused. Vampires with pyrokinesis have on occasion accidentally incinerated themselves as we are vulnerable to fire.

Perhaps the greatest limitation of our powers is their dependence on blood. Without regular feeding, our abilities weaken and fade. Without the life force of regular infusions we become little more than shadows of our true selves. This dependency is a constant reminder of the delicate balance we must maintain.

Stories of Power

I recall a night in Paris when I used mesmerism to save myself from discovery. A detective had been following me, his suspicions aroused by a string of unexplained disappearances. I had nothing to do with them I assure you. He cornered me in an alley, his hand resting on the hilt of a silver dagger. "You're not human," he said, his voice steady but his eyes betraying his fear.

I met his gaze and spoke softly. "You've made a mistake. You were following someone else." His grip on the dagger loosened as the suggestion took hold. I continued, weaving a story of a shadowy figure disappearing into the night. By the time I was done, he was convinced that he had been chasing a phantom. He left the alley, muttering apologies, and I slipped away unseen.

Another time, I used shadow manipulation to infiltrate a heavily guarded mansion. A rival vampire had stolen an artifact of great importance to my brethren, and it was my task to retrieve it. Moving through the shadows, I evaded guards and security cameras, my form blending seamlessly with the darkness. When I reached the artifact, I felt a surge of triumph. The return journey was just as smooth, and by dawn, the artifact was safely back in my brethren's possession.

Reflections on Power

Our powers are tools, not toys. They are gifts that come with responsibility, for their misuse can have dire consequences. I have seen vampires consumed by their abilities, their arrogance leading to their downfall. Power, after all, is a double-edged sword.

For me, these abilities are a means to an end. They allow me to survive, to protect those I care about, and to maintain the delicate balance between our world and the human one. But I never forget the price of these gifts—the hunger, the isolation, and the eternal vigilance they demand.

Vampire powers are as much a part of us as our fangs or our need for blood. They define us, shape us, and remind us of what we are. And while they set us apart from humanity, they also bind us to it, for every power we wield comes with a responsibility to use it wisely. In the end, it is not the powers themselves that define us, but how we choose to wield them.

Chapter 20
From the Writings of A Fledgling Vampire
Found in an Abandoned Hotel Room: Entry 10

I don't know who I am anymore. Or what I am.

It started last night, or was it the night before? Time feels strange now, slippery, like it's no longer anchored to me. I woke up in the alley where I last remember being alive. My throat burned like I'd swallowed fire, and my body ached in ways I didn't think possible. But I wasn't dead. No, I was something worse.

The first thing I noticed was the hunger. It's not like being hungry for food; it's deeper, sharper, like every cell in my body is screaming for something I can't name. Then I smelled it—blood. A man passed by, his arm scraped and bleeding. The scent hit me like a drug, and before I knew what I was doing, I was moving toward him.

I didn't hurt him; I couldn't. But I wanted to. God help me, I wanted to.

Today, I tested myself, desperate to understand what I've become. My reflection in the mirror is different. My eyes catch the light in a way they never did before, like polished obsidian. My skin is paler, smoother, and almost luminous. And I'm strong. I crushed a piece of brick in my hand like it was chalk.

The sun hurts. Even the weak winter light stings my skin and makes my head throb. I had to retreat to the shadows, where the burning eased.

But the strangest thing is the way the world feels now. Every sound is sharp and clear. I can hear the rustle of leaves, as well as the hum of a distant car engine. I can hear the heartbeat of the woman in the apartment above me. I can smell the salt of her sweat, the coppery tang of her blood.

I should be terrified. I should hate this. But a part of me doesn't. A part of me feels... powerful.

And that scares me most of all.

I had survived the first few days of my new existence, though 'survived' hardly seemed the right word. I was a monster, a creature of the night, and my every instinct was a reminder of the darkness I carried within me. The hunger was a constant companion, a gnawing ache that no amount of rationalization could suppress. I was a vampire, and with that realization came a freedom wrapped in chains.

The night was my domain now, and as I walked the quiet streets, I felt the pull of my new nature. The city was alive with light and sound, but it was the shadows that called to me. They promised me the anonymity I desperately needed.

I came upon a young woman, her laughter cutting through the night. I followed her, my heightened senses tuned to her every move. She stumbled, her steps hindered by the late hour and the drinks she had consumed. It was a perfect opportunity, and I acted without thought for her well-being.

The encounter was brutal and clumsy. My fangs found their mark, but my inexperience was evident. I tore at her skin in my desperation, my need overwhelming any semblance of control. She cried out, a sound that cut through me, haunting and terrible. I left her there, her lifeblood spilled on the cold pavement, a testament to my monstrous act.

As I fled the scene, a shop window caught my attention. The glass was dark, mirrored, and as I gazed upon my reflection, I saw the truth of what I had become. My image was faint, almost ethereal. I was fading, becoming something other than what I once was. The realization was chilling, and I knew that my transformation was not yet complete.

I was being watched, tracked by those who understood the true nature of the creatures that roamed the night. The Rose and Raven Society, with their silver blades and unwavering faith, had marked me as a threat to be eliminated. I had become too reckless, too careless, and now I was to pay the ultimate price.

They cornered me in an alley, their faces hidden by the shadows of the night. I could hear their hearts beating, smell the determination in their every move. They spoke of justice, of protection, but all I felt was the cold grip of fear. I was no match for them, not like this.

The end came swiftly, a sharp pain followed by a fleeting moment of weightlessness as I fell to the cold, hard ground. My last thoughts were not of regret but of a woman, a vampire like me, who had loved me in my final moments. She had been my end, my own personal angel of death, and in her embrace, I found a strange sort of peace.

The agent of the Rose and Raven Society who found me in my apartment, who investigated my final days, wrote of me with a mix of reverence and disgust. I was a cautionary tale, a reminder of the dangers that lurked in the shadows. But she was there too, the vampire who had turned me, who had loved me in her own way.

She was there, a shadow among shadows, as the agent recounted the last moments of my human life. She loved me, in her way, and she mourned me as only those who walk in darkness can. Her love was a violent, consuming thing, and in her arms, I found my end.

Chapter 21
Our History

Shadows Through Time: The History of Vampires

The history of vampires is a story written in the margins of human history, a tale of shadows and whispers that has shaped the world in ways most mortals will never know. We have been here since the dawn of civilization, watching, influencing, and surviving. While humanity records its wars, revolutions, and renaissances, our contributions are hidden, etched in the bloodlines we have touched and the legends we have left behind.

Vampires and Human Society

Our relationship with humanity has always been symbiotic. Humans are our sustenance, but they are also our greatest threat. For centuries, we have lived among you, adapting to your customs, adopting your languages, and shaping your cultures. In ancient times, vampires were often revered as gods or feared as demons. The rulers of early civilizations—Egyptian pharaohs, Mesopotamian kings, and Mayan priests—sometimes counted vampires among their ranks, our immortality lending an air of divinity to their reigns.

During the Middle Ages, as religion tightened its grip on Europe, vampires became the stuff of nightmares. The Church declared us abominations, and witch hunts often extended to suspected vampires. This era forced us into deeper hiding, but it also sharpened our survival instincts. We learned to manipulate human institutions, influencing politics and economics from the shadows.

The Enlightenment brought with it a new fascination with the supernatural. Writers and philosophers speculated about our existence, turning us into figures of intrigue rather than fear. By the 19th century, vampires had become romanticized, thanks in part to works like Bram Stoker's *Dracula*. Little did Stoker know, his fictional creation was inspired by real figures—vampires who had walked the earth long before his time. Dracula, by the way, was a real son of a bitch!

Famous Vampires in History

Much of history's most enigmatic figures were, in fact, vampires. Take Vlad the Impaler, one of the inspirations for Stoker's

Dracula. While much of his legend is exaggerated, Vlad was indeed a vampire. He ruled his land with an iron fist, feeding on the blood of his enemies and instilling fear that still lingers in the Carpathian Mountains.

Elizabeth Báthory, the Blood Countess, is another infamous figure. History remembers her as a human noblewoman who bathed in the blood of virgins to preserve her youth. The truth is both simpler and darker: she was a vampire who used her noble status to mask her feeding habits. Her excesses eventually drew too much attention, leading to her downfall.

Not all famous vampires were tyrants. In the Renaissance, a vampire named Lorenzo was a patron of the arts in Florence. His wealth and influence helped usher in an era of unparalleled creativity. Lorenzo's brethren worked behind the scenes, ensuring that the Medici family maintained power, all while feeding discreetly on the city's underworld.

Encounters with Vampires from the Past

I have had the privilege—and sometimes the misfortune—of meeting many of these historical figures. One of the most memorable was an encounter with Elizabeth Báthory. It was the late 16th century, and I had traveled to her castle under the guise of a wandering scholar. I had heard rumors of her activities and sought to warn her of the danger she was courting.

Elizabeth was as captivating as she was ruthless. Her beauty was otherworldly, her manner regal, but her eyes betrayed a darkness that even I found unsettling. I remember her sweet, sickening voice as she said to me: "You judge me," her voice like silk. "But we are the same, you and I."

"No," I replied. "I take only what I need. You take for pleasure."

She laughed, a sound both musical and chilling. "Pleasure is the only thing that makes eternity bearable."

Our conversation ended abruptly when her servants interrupted, dragging in a young girl who looked no older than fifteen. I left that night, knowing there was no saving her. Months later, news of her arrest reached me. Even vampires are not immune to the consequences of hubris.

Reflections on Vampire History

The history of vampires is a mirror to human history, reflecting both its triumphs and its tragedies. We have been warriors and poets, tyrants and benefactors. We have shaped empires and watched them crumble, always adapting, always surviving.

Yet, for all our power and longevity, we remain bound by the same forces that govern humanity: the need to belong, the fear of discovery, and the relentless passage of time. Our history is a testament to our resilience, but it is also a reminder of our fragility.

As I walk through the modern world, I see echoes of the past in every corner. The skyscrapers of New York remind me of the towers of Florence; the hum of technology recalls the whispers of ancient courts. We are still here, woven into the fabric of your history, watching, waiting, and surviving in the shadows. For as long as humanity endures, so too shall we.

Chapter 22
An Account of My Meeting Bram Stoker And the Vampire Sir Henry Irving Early 1900s

Tonight, I walked among mortals more keenly aware of my nature than I have been in centuries. The Lyceum Theatre was a blaze of light and life, its halls filled with the chatter of London's elite. I had come to observe, to amuse myself with their trivialities. Instead, I found myself in the company of two men who, unknowingly, have immortalized me.

Sir Henry Irving was everything the rumors claimed: tall, commanding, his every gesture deliberate, as though he were always performing. His presence drew the eyes of all, and yet he noticed me. I knew it the moment his gaze lingered, sharp and appraising. Did he sense something? A predator recognizing another?

Then there was Stoker. Less imposing, but no less intriguing. He hovered at Irving's side, deferential yet observant, his eyes darting about the room as if cataloging every detail for later use. When Irving introduced us, Stoker's handshake was firm, his smile genuine.

"Have we met before?" he asked, his tone polite but curious.

"No," I replied, smiling just enough to unsettle him. "But I know of you, Mr. Stoker. Your book has caused quite a stir."

He flushed at the compliment, though whether from pride or discomfort, I could not tell. "Alas, it has sold little, and I do not count it a success. You are speaking of the vampire book, correct?"

Yes, "Dracula," I continued, savoring the way the name lingered on my tongue. "A fascinating tale. You've captured the essence of something ancient, though I suspect you've never seen it with your own eyes."

Stoker laughed nervously, but Irving's gaze sharpened. I could feel his curiosity, his suspicion.

As the evening wore on, I found myself drawn into their circle. Stoker spoke of his inspirations, of folklore and fears, while Irving watched me with the intensity of a hawk. I left before they could learn too much, but not before whispering a parting thought to Stoker:

"Beware, Mr. Stoker. Some truths are best left in the shadows."

He looked pale as I departed, and I confess, I enjoyed it. Let them wonder. Let them dream. After all, I am the very thing they seek to understand.

Chapter 23
Rogue Vampires

The Shadow of Rogue Vampires

If you have read this far, you now realize that vampires have existed alongside humanity for millennia, hidden in plain sight. Most of us live by an unspoken code: take only what we need, leave no trace, and protect the delicate balance that allows us to coexist with the mortal world. But not all vampires adhere to this code. Rogue vampires—those who kill indiscriminately and revel in chaos—are the reason humans fear us, the reason the word "vampire" conjures images of monsters and nightmares.

The Rogue Threat

Rogue vampires are a threat to more than just humans; they endanger all of us. Their actions draw attention, leaving behind bodies and evidence that even the most unskilled hunters can follow. They are predators without restraint, driven by hunger, hatred, or madness. Some revel in the power of their immortality, seeing humans as nothing more than prey. Others are newly turned and unable to control their urges, their humanity stripped away by the overwhelming need to feed.

For centuries, rogue vampires have been the greatest challenge to our survival. Every time one of them kills, they leave a mark that ripples through both human and vampire society. Hunters are emboldened, governments whisper of conspiracies, and our carefully maintained secrecy begins to unravel.

Encounters with Killers

I have encountered rogue vampires on several occasions, and each experience has left me shaken. The first time was in the slums of 19th-century London. I had been tracking rumors of a vampire who was killing prostitutes, leaving their bodies drained and discarded in alleyways. The humans called him Jack the Ripper, but we knew better. His name was Darius, a rogue who had abandoned the code long ago.

When I found him, he was standing over his latest victim, his face smeared with blood, his eyes wild with madness. "You shouldn't be here," he snarled, baring his fangs.

"You've made this everyone's problem," I replied, stepping closer. "Do you have any idea what you've done?"

Darius laughed, a hollow, bitter sound. "They're just cattle. Who cares what happens to them?"

I didn't hesitate. Rogue vampires cannot be reasoned with, and every moment they live is another risk to our kind. The fight was brutal, his strength fueled by years of unrestrained feeding. But in the end, I drove a silver blade through his heart and left his body to burn in the morning sun.

Another encounter occurred in modern-day Los Angeles. A young vampire named Serena had gone rogue after being abandoned by her sire. She was new, frightened, and dangerous, leaving a trail of bodies in her wake. I found her in a derelict warehouse, trembling and covered in blood.

"I didn't mean to," she whispered, her voice barely audible. "I couldn't stop."

I saw the desperation in her eyes, the remnants of humanity struggling against the monster she had become. Instead of killing her, I took her under my wing, teaching her how to control her hunger. It wasn't easy, and there were moments when I doubted my decision. But Serena eventually learned restraint, and she now works to help other fledglings avoid her mistakes.

Why Humans Fear Us

Rogue vampires are the embodiment of humanity's worst fears. They are the monsters in the dark, the predators who prey on the vulnerable. Their actions feed the myths and legends that have haunted human imagination for centuries. And while most of us strive to live in harmony with the mortal world, the damage done by rogues is difficult to undo.

The fear they inspire is not unfounded. To humans, a vampire is a creature of immense power, capable of killing with ease and vanishing without a trace. The stories of rogue vampires—of villages wiped out, families torn apart, and bodies left drained of blood—are enough to make anyone fear the night.

Lessons from the Rogues

Rogue vampires are a cautionary tale, a reminder of what happens when power is unchecked, and instincts are left unrestrained. They are the reason we have rules, the reason we must police our own kind. For every rogue who is stopped, countless lives—human and vampire—are saved.

But they also serve as a reminder of our own fragility. Every vampire has the potential to go rogue, to lose themselves to hunger or despair. It is a constant battle, one that requires discipline and purpose. Without those, we risk becoming the very monsters humans believe us to be.

A Plea for Understanding

To those who read this, I ask only for understanding. Not all vampires are killers. Most of us live quietly, taking only what we need and striving to coexist with humanity. But the actions of a few have painted us all as monsters. If you ever encounter a vampire, remember that we are not defined by the rogues among us.

We are individuals, each with our own choices, struggles, and humanity—however faint it may seem.

The night is vast, and its shadows are deep. But not all who walk in darkness are lost. Some of us are simply trying to survive, to find meaning in an eternal existence. And for every rogue who threatens that balance, there are others who fight to preserve it.

Chapter 24
From the Writings of
Ebenezer Smith
Rose and Raven Vampire Hunter: 1791

I had been tracking the rogue for weeks, following the trail of drained livestock and missing villagers. This one was different from the others I've faced. It was cunning, deliberate, as if it enjoyed the chase as much as the kill. Tonight, in the crumbling remains of an abandoned mill, it finally revealed itself.

The place reeked of decay. People observing the vampire might mistake that it was female. They would be wrong, It is an it. Broken beams jutted out of the broken mill, and the air was thick with the metallic tang of blood. My every step echoed, a betrayal of my presence, but I pressed on, crossbow at the ready.

It struck without warning, a blur of shadow and malice. I was thrown against the wall, the impact knocking the breath from my lungs. When I looked up, it stood before me. It was a creature both monstrous and eerily human. Its eyes burned with a feral light, and its lips curled into a smile that bared those cursed fangs. One of its breasts hung out of it's torn clothing. It might have been an enticement to some, but to me it was an abomination. Still, as feral as it was, I could see the beauty it might have had once and I felt a strange sensation to— no! I can't let my mind go there. I looked for my crossbow. It had been knocked out of my hands.

"You've been following me," it said, its voice a low, mocking purr. "Do you enjoy the hunt as much as I do?"

"I do!" I said. I am no stranger to the wiles of women, but the hunger in its eyes was unlike anything I had ever encountered. There was a wildness to it, an untamed ferocity that both terrified and enthralled me. I reminded myself that I was Ebenezer Smith, a hunter of its kind, and yet, in that moment, I found myself faltering.

The crossbow lay just beyond my reach, its shaft glinting in the scant moonlight that filtered through the broken roof. I had faced many vampires in my time, but none had ever caught me so off-guard, so utterly unprepared for the battle at hand.

"Do you think yourself worthy of such prey?" I managed to choke out, my voice steady despite the fear that gnawed at my insides.

It laughed with a sound that seemed too pure, too alive, to come from such a monstrous being. "Worthy?" it echoed, tilting its head to one side as it regarded me with a mixture of amusement and curiosity. "You are different from the others. They scream and plead. But you... you stand your ground even now."

I pushed myself up into a sitting position, wincing as pain lanced through my battered body. "I've dedicated my life to eradicating your kind," I said, meeting its gaze with a defiance born of years spent in the shadows, tracking the creatures of the night.

The vampire stepped closer, its movements fluid and predatory. "And yet, here you are, at my mercy," it murmured, its eyes roaming over me with an intensity that gave me intense anxiety. "Tell me, Ebenezer Smith, what drives a man to such pursuits? Is it a thirst for vengeance? A misguided sense of duty?"

It knew my name. "You wouldn't understand," I replied, my hand inching towards the crossbow, fingers grazing the cool metal of its stock.

"Try me," it said, closing the distance between us in the blink of an eye. Before I could react, it was upon me, its body pressing against mine with an intimacy that left me both repulsed and captivated.

The world seemed to narrow to this singular moment, this dangerous dance with death itself. The vampire's lips hovered just above mine, its breath mingling with my own as it whispered, "Let go, hunter. Embrace the darkness. I can feel you want to."

And in that moment of weakness, I did. I reached for it, pulling it closer as our lips met in a kiss that was both a betrayal of my mission and a surrender to the primal hunger that coursed through my veins. It was a kiss that bridged the chasm between predator and prey, a moment of macabre beauty in a world defined by bloodshed and horror.

But the embrace was short-lived. As quickly as it had begun, it ended with a sharp intake of breath from the vampire. It pulled back, its eyes wide with what might have been surprise or perhaps even disappointment.

"You are not like them," it said, a note of regret in its voice. "There is a strength in you, a purity of purpose that I did not expect."

I felt a sudden surge of clarity, the haze of desire lifted from my mind. Had it glamoured me?

"And yet," I countered, "you still mean to kill me."

The vampire's expression hardened. "It is the nature of our existence, hunter. I am sorry."

With a speed that belied its grace, the vampire's fangs sank into my neck, the pain a stark reminder of the reality I had momentarily forgotten. I struggled against it, but my efforts were in vain. The world around me began to darken as the creature fed on me, draining the life from my body.

As consciousness slipped away, my thoughts turned to the irony of my fate. I, who had spent my life hunting the undead, had fallen victim to the very creatures I sought to destroy. And yet, there was no fear in me, only a profound sense of acceptance.

I awoke to the cold light of dawn, the vampire gone, leaving behind nothing but the echo of its presence. My body ached with a weariness that seemed to seep into my very bones, and I knew that my time as a hunter had come to an end.

In the days that followed, I pondered the events that had unfolded in that cursed mill. The rogue vampire had used its femininity to disarm me, to lure me into a false sense of security.

It was a lesson that I would carry with me for the rest of my days, however few remained.

As I penned my final journal entry, I reflected on the perilous dance between humans and vampires. It was a dance fraught with danger and desire, a delicate balance that could so easily be tipped into chaos and destruction.

—Ebenezer Smith 18 July 1791

The tale of Ebenezer Smith stands as a cautionary reminder: that to embrace the darkness is to invite madness, and that the line between hunter and hunted can be frightfully thin. Let it be known that the allure of the vampire can ensnare even the most steadfast of hearts, and that the cost of such folly is often more than one is willing to pay.

The rogue vampire, a creature of both horror and exquisite beauty, remains at large, a testament to the cunning and resilience of its kind. It is a reminder that in the world of the supernatural, not all monsters lurk in the shadows, and not all angels are sent from heaven.

Hunters of Vampires, heed my words, Do not let your guard down, nor let your heart be swayed by the siren song of the undead. For in the end, it is not the strength of your arm that will save you, but the resolve of your will and the clarity of your purpose.

And remember this: the beauty of the vampire is but a veil, concealing the rot that lies beneath. Do not be fooled by the illusion, for to do so may well cost you your life, or worse, your very soul. But I know these words will fall on deaf ears and blind eyes. — Sabastian Wolfram 10 October 1975

Chapter 25
Famous Vampire Hunter Accounts

The Eternal Adversary: Vampire Hunters

For as long as vampires have existed, there have been those who seek to destroy us. Vampire hunters are our eternal adversaries, a force as relentless as time itself. They are the shadow to our darkness, the human response to the fear and fascination we inspire. Their history is as old as ours, their methods evolving alongside us. To be a vampire is to live with the constant threat of discovery and the knowledge that somewhere, someone is always hunting.

The History of Vampire Hunters

The origins of vampire hunters can be traced back to the earliest civilizations. In ancient Mesopotamia, priests would conduct rituals to banish "blood demons," likely inspired by early encounters with vampires. In Egypt, hunters were often temple guards, wielding blessed weapons to protect the living from what they called "eternal feeders."

The Middle Ages marked a turning point. As the Church consolidated power in Europe, it declared vampires to be agents of the devil. This era saw the rise of organized hunting orders, such as the Order of Saint Michael, whose members were trained to identify and eliminate vampires. These hunters were equipped with holy relics, silver weapons, and the authority of the Church, making them formidable foes.

The Enlightenment brought a shift in tactics. Vampire hunters began to rely on science and reason rather than superstition. They studied our weaknesses, developing new weapons and strategies. By the 19th century, hunters were using everything from alchemical potions to early firearms loaded with silver bullets.

Today, vampire hunters are more dangerous than ever. They are no longer bound by religious dogma or outdated methods. Modern hunters use technology—thermal imaging, DNA analysis, and even drones—to track us. They are organized, resourceful, and relentless, operating in secret to avoid the scrutiny of human authorities.

Famous Vampire Hunters

Throughout history, certain hunters have gained legendary status among both their kind and ours. One such figure was Abraham Van Helsing, whose exploits against Dracula were immortalized in fiction. While Stoker's account is embellished, Van Helsing was a real man—a scientist and theologian who dedicated his life to eradicating vampires. His methods were meticulous, combining ancient lore with modern science. Some of our kind have even alluded to the supposition that he was able to wield magic. Some believe he is still among us, or his ancestors, and he is still hunting.

Another infamous hunter was Elizabeth Grayson, a Victorian-era aristocrat who turned her wealth and influence into a personal crusade against vampires. She was known for her ruthlessness and cunning, often infiltrating vampire covens to destroy them from within. Grayson was eventually killed in a confrontation with a vampire elder, but her legacy endures.

In more recent times, the name Dominic Kessler strikes fear into our kind. A former military operative, Kessler leads a covert organization known as the Black Cross. His team is equipped with advanced weaponry and has been responsible for the destruction of several vampire communities. Kessler is methodical and cold, viewing us not as monsters but as threats to be neutralized.

Encounters with Vampire Hunters

Since the first days of my keeping this journal when I had only encountered a hunter once, I have unfortunately faced hunters on many more occasions. Each encounter has left its mark. One of the most harrowing occurred in Prague during the mid 20th century. A group of hunters, led by a man named Viktor Halek, had been tracking me for weeks. Halek was a former priest turned hunter, his faith unshaken despite leaving the Church.

One night, they ambushed me in an abandoned cathedral. The attack was brutal and calculated. They used fire to drive me out into the open, forcing me to fight on their terms. I remember the searing pain of a silver blade cutting into my arm, the acrid smell of burning wood and holy oil. With some difficulty, I managed to escape. Two of my brethren were not so lucky. I hear they were killed mercilessly, their ashes scattered among the ruins.

Another encounter, more recent, occurred in New York. A lone hunter, armed with ultraviolet grenades and a crossbow, had been stalking me for weeks. He was young and inexperienced but determined. When he finally confronted me, I disarmed him easily, but I didn't kill him. Instead, I erased his memory of me and left him alive, hoping he might abandon his quest. Whether he did or not, I never found out.

The Methods of Attack

Hunters are nothing if not resourceful. Their methods vary widely, depending on their training and resources. Some rely on traditional weapons like stakes, silver blades, and holy water. Others use modern innovations, such as ultraviolet light emitters, incendiary rounds, and chemical agents designed to weaken us.

One of the most dangerous tactics is psychological warfare. Hunters have been known to spread rumors or plant evidence to turn humans against us. They exploit our need for secrecy, knowing that exposure is often as deadly as their weapons.

Reflections on the Hunt

Vampire hunters are both a curse and a catalyst. They are a constant reminder of our vulnerabilities, forcing us to remain vigilant and adaptable. While I despise their methods, I cannot entirely blame them. To them, we are predators, threats to their existence.

Yet, for all their efforts, hunters will never truly eradicate us. We are too resilient, too adaptable, and too many in number. As long as humans fear the night, as long as blood flows through their veins, we will endure. And so the dance continues, an eternal struggle between predator and prey, hunter and hunted.

For those of us who walk the shadows, the threat of hunters is a part of life—an adversary we respect, even as we strive to outwit them.

Chapter 26
Journal Entry of John Stanley
November 3, 1896

The frost clings to my coat, the air sharp as daggers against my skin. I sit here, by the dim light of a flickering lantern, my hand trembling, but it is not from the cold, but from what I've just endured. Tonight, I faced one of them. Not a creature of myth or superstition, but a true vampire.

The hunt began as most do: whispers in the tavern, a farmer's daughter gone missing, and livestock found drained of blood. The signs were unmistakable. I tracked the creature to the ruins of an old chapel deep in the forest. Its stained-glass windows were shattered, and the altar lay in ruins, desecrated by time and, perhaps, by the evil that had claimed it.

I waited in silence, my crossbow loaded with a silver-tipped bolt, my heart pounding in my ears. The hours dragged on until, at last, it emerged.

It was nothing like the stories. No flowing cape or noble visage. This was a predator, lean and feral, its eyes glowing faintly in the moonlight like embers in a dying fire. Its movements were unnaturally smooth, as if it floated rather than walked. It smiled at me, revealing fangs that glinted like knives.

The fight was swift and brutal. It lunged, faster than I could react, and I barely managed to roll aside. My bolt struck its shoulder, but it didn't stop. The creature hissed, its voice a guttural growl that echoed in my skull. We grappled, and I drove a silver dagger into its chest. It shrieked with a sound so unearthly it felt as though the forest itself recoiled.

It fled into the shadows, leaving behind a trail of black ichor. I am alive, but I know this is far from over. It will heal, and it will return.

God help me.

It did return from what I heard. God was not on Mr. Stanley's side.

Chapter 27
Vampire Legends

The Truth Behind the Legends

The truth is that vampires have existed for as long as humans have told stories. We are the shadow in the corner of your vision, the whisper in the dark, the inexplicable chill on an otherwise warm night. But the tales you tell about us—those legends and myths—are only fragments of the truth. They are reflections of our existence, distorted by fear, imagination, and the passage of time. As a vampire, I've often wondered how these stories came to be and how they've shaped both human and vampire culture.

The Origins of Vampire Myths

The first vampire legends emerged long before the word "vampire" existed. In ancient Mesopotamia, the *ekimmu* were restless spirits that fed on the living, and the *Lamashtu* was a demon said to drink the blood of infants. These early tales likely stemmed from a fear of death and the unknown, but they also hint at encounters with creatures like us—beings who lived in the shadows and fed on life itself.

In Eastern Europe, the vampire as we know it began to take shape. The *strigoi* of Romanian folklore were undead beings who rose from their graves to drink the blood of the living. These legends often arose in times of plague, when unexplained deaths and uncorrupted corpses led to superstitions about the dead returning to life. Villagers would exhume bodies, drive stakes through their hearts, or burn them to prevent further "attacks."

The myths spread and evolved as cultures merged. In Greece, the *vrykolakas*, which is a word more closely related to werewolf than vampire, were cursed souls who preyed on their families. In Asia, the Chinese *jiangshi* were hopping vampires that drained life energy rather than blood. Each culture added its own fears and beliefs to the vampire mythos, creating a patchwork of stories that still persist today.

Note from the editor, Beckett Blaise: I have written a Book of Vampires called "What Hunts You at Night." It has much more information about the *jiangshi* as well as information about all vampire myths. It is available for purchase now.

Influence on Vampire Culture

These legends have shaped not only how humans perceive us but also how we perceive ourselves. For centuries, vampires have used these myths to their advantage, perpetuating falsehoods to confuse and mislead. The idea that we cannot cross running water, for instance, was likely spread by an ancient brethren to deter hunters from pursuing them across rivers. The belief that garlic repels us is partially true. The natural curative properties of garlic work in a similar fashion to the way silver harms us. The purity and healing power of garlic can do great harm to the undead.

Here are some other beliefs that indeed do hold a bit of sway over us. The idea that sunlight harms us is not entirely inaccurate. While we do not burst into flames, prolonged exposure weakens us significantly, leaving us vulnerable. The connection between vampires and bats is also rooted in reality; many of us feel a kinship with these nocturnal creatures, and some even adopt their imagery as part of their identity.

Within vampire culture, these legends serve as a reminder of our dual existence. We are both predators and prey, feared and hunted by those who create these stories. The myths bind us together, a shared history that transcends time and geography.

Encounters with the Unknown

Not all creatures of the night are vampires, though many have been mistaken for us. I once encountered a being in the Carpathian Mountains that defied explanation. It was a cold winter night, and I was tracking a human who had strayed too far from the safety of their village. As I moved through the forest, I sensed another presence—a predator, but not one of my kind.

The creature emerged from the shadows, its form humanoid but twisted. Its eyes glowed faintly, and its breath came in ragged gasps that clouded the frigid air. It moved with a speed and grace that rivaled my own, and when it spoke, its voice was a guttural rasp.

"You are not welcome here," it said, its tone more warning than threat.

"What are you?" I asked, genuinely curious.

"A guardian," it replied, before disappearing into the darkness.

I never saw it again, but the encounter stayed with me. Was it a *strigoi*, as the villagers whispered? Or something older, something forgotten by both humans and vampires? I do not know, but it reminded me that the world is vast and filled with mysteries even we cannot fully understand.

Another time, in 19th-century Paris, I met a woman who claimed to be a *lamia*. She was strikingly beautiful, her movements serpentine, her presence magnetic. She spoke of ancient Greece, of feeding not on blood but on desire and despair. Whether she was truly a lamia or simply a vampire who had adopted the myth, I could not tell. But her stories were haunting, filled with the echoes of lives she had touched and destroyed.

The Power of Stories

The legends humans tell about vampires are more than just tales; they are a reflection of your fears and desires, your need to explain the unexplainable. For us, they are both a shield and a mirror, shaping how we navigate your world and how we see ourselves.

As I write this, I wonder what new myths will arise in the centuries to come. Will humans continue to fear us, or will they come to understand the truth behind the stories? Perhaps it doesn't matter. For as long as the night exists, so too will the legends. And in those legends, we will endure—immortal, unyielding, and forever intertwined with the dreams and nightmares of humanity.

Chapter 28
Personal Encounter
Sabastian Wolfram
April 23, 1927

The woods tonight were restless, the kind of silence that pricks at one's instincts and makes even the immortal cautious. I have hunted in these forests for centuries, their paths as familiar to me as the lines on my palm. Yet tonight, something was different.

The moon was veiled by heavy clouds, and the wind carried a scent I could not place—earthy, metallic, and sharp, like the tang of blood mixed with rusted iron. I followed it, curious but wary. Hunger drove me forward, but a deeper instinct whispered caution.

I found it near a clearing, crouched over the remains of some unfortunate creature. At first, I thought it a wolf, but as I drew closer, I realized how wrong I was. Its shape was fluid, shifting in the shadows as though it couldn't decide what form to take.

Eyes, glowing a sickly yellow, snapped to meet mine. They were not the eyes of prey.

It stood, its form stretching unnaturally tall, limbs too long, its body cloaked in darkness that seemed to writhe and breathe. It made no sound, but the air between us felt alive with malice.

I spoke, though I am not sure why. "What are you?"

It tilted its head, a grotesque mimicry of human curiosity, and then it smiled. Not a friendly smile, but a gaping maw lined with teeth that seemed to go on forever.

When it lunged, I moved faster, darting into the trees. I am no stranger to fear, but this... this was something primal. It gave chase, silent and relentless, until I lost it in a thicket where the shadows were thickest.

I sit now in the hollow of an old oak, writing these words as the night stretches on. I am not alone in these woods, and whatever hunts here is no mere beast.

I wonder, for the first time in centuries, if I have met something older than myself. Something I cannot kill.

Chapter 29
Our Survival

Lessons in Immortality: Reflections of a Vampire

Yes, I have walked the earth for centuries, a silent observer to the rise and fall of empires, the ebb and flow of human life. To be a vampire is to live on the fringes of existence, neither fully a part of the world nor entirely apart from it. Our survival is a testament to our adaptability, our cunning, and our capacity to endure. But it is not without its challenges, and the lessons I have learned are as much about humanity as they are about myself.

Reflections on Survival

The first lesson I learned as a vampire was restraint. The hunger is relentless, a gnawing need that can easily overwhelm even the strongest will. In my early years, I gave in too often, feeding recklessly and leaving behind a trail of suspicion and fear. It wasn't long before hunters came for me, forcing me to flee and start anew. It was a harsh but necessary reminder that survival depends on discipline. To be a vampire is to live with constant temptation, and mastering it is the key to enduring the centuries.

Another lesson is the importance of discretion. We are creatures of the night, and secrecy is our greatest defense. The modern world is far less forgiving than it was in the past. Cameras, forensic science, and the interconnectedness of humanity mean that even the smallest mistake can lead to exposure. I have learned to blend in, to move unnoticed through the world, leaving no trace of my presence. It is a lonely existence at times, but it is the price of survival.

Perhaps the most profound lesson is the value of perspective. Time changes everything, and as the years stretch into centuries, you begin to see the world differently. The petty concerns of mortals fade into insignificance, replaced by a deeper understanding of the cycles that govern life. Wars, plagues, revolutions—they are all temporary, mere moments in the grand tapestry of history. This perspective is both a blessing and a curse, for it can lead to detachment, a sense of disconnection from the world. But it can also bring clarity and purpose, if you let it.

Advice for the Curious

To those who may one day encounter a vampire, I offer this advice: approach us with caution but not with fear. We are not the monsters of legend, nor are we the romantic figures of fiction. We are beings of complexity, shaped by our experiences and our choices. If you meet one of us, remember that we are not so different from you. We have desires, fears, and regrets, just as you do. But also remember that we are predators, and our survival often depends on your ignorance.

For those who might consider becoming a vampire, I urge you to think carefully. Immortality is not the gift it appears to be. It is a burden, a test of endurance that few can pass. You will lose the life you knew, the people you loved, and the simplicity of mortality. In exchange, you will gain power, perspective, and the chance to witness history unfold. It is a trade-off, and only you can decide if it is worth it.

Keeping an Open Mind

The idea of vampires may seem far-fetched, a relic of superstition and folklore. But I ask you to consider this: the world is vast, and there is much that remains unexplained. Vampires are real, and we have been here all along, watching from the shadows. We are not asking for acceptance or understanding, only that you keep an open mind. The next time you feel a chill in the night or sense a presence you cannot explain, remember that the world is more mysterious than you know.

For me, survival is not just about feeding or avoiding discovery. It is about finding meaning in a life without end, about embracing the darkness while holding onto a sliver of light. And perhaps, in sharing my story, I can help you see that the line between human and vampire is not as clear as it seems. We are not so different, after all. Both of us are simply trying to survive in a world that is both beautiful and cruel.

Chapter 30
What I Know About This Vampire named Sabastian Wolfram so Far
Beckett Blaise: Present Day

Even as the vampire spoke of peaceful coexistence, if one looks deep enough into the writing contained within the pages of this diary, one can see the lies and the cover ups. He is a killer. Make no mistake of that. One needs to look no further than his account of dispatching the one he said we called Jack the Ripper. His account of the killing of his own kind reverberates his methods and reveals his skill in brutality.

I don't know if I have ever heard of a morally sound vampire. They may start out as an innocent victim of some unscrupulous vampire sire, but as the hunger and the lifestyle of the vampire permeates their lives, or unlives, they reveal their true natures, that of brutal, ruthless killers and predators. I have been watching Wolfram, who is often referred to as 'Wolfy' for quite some time. I have conversed with his biographer, Seth Aubrey, and interviewed a few of his victims, the ones who lived, and I have concluded this journal is propaganda designed to make the reader believe he is some misunderstood dupe who was in the wrong place at the wrong time. Nothing can be further from the truth. Let me tell you the story I heard about his turning.

First, there was no hulking male sire who took him by the neck unwillingly. Wolfy was turned by a woman. The account of what year this occurred is unknown, but from my research is was in the late fifteen hundreds when Shakespeare was writing and producing his now famous plays. Wolfram was in love with a woman who endeavored to be an actress at a time when females were forbidden to act in the theatre. She would throw herself at the owners of the Blackfriars Theatre, the Rose, the Swan and finally the Globe where Shakespeare presented his plays. They all had their way with her according to my sources which infuriated Wolfram.

I am paraphrasing to get the point, but in the early sixteen hundreds he followed her around pleading for her affections until Shakespeare himself began a torrid affair with her. She disappeared later on, and Wolfram feared she was dead. He had it in his mind that the King's Men, or so they would be called later if they were not called that already, killed her so he burned down the Globe Theatre in 1613.

Destitute and depressed, Wolfram roamed from place to place until he, at last, ended up in Paris, France. That's where he met up with the woman again. (I still don't know her exact name) He rekindled his love for her only now she had become a woman of the night, and I don't mean a prostitute. She was a vampire. She toyed with him and finally turned him.

If you notice in this journal, he often talks about occurrences in Paris. That's because he spent a lot of time there. He doesn't want anyone to know the truth, so he invented the story about being taken as a vampire against his will and hating the man who did it. He talks about hunting down the vampire and taking his revenge. A good story but a false one. The fact is he pleaded with the woman he had been chasing to turn him so he could be with her forever. She finally agreed and then promptly she left him for parts unknown. The only truth to his sire story is that he still hunts for his maker, he does. But it is this woman he hunts.

All these centuries later he is still looking for her. He has found her a few times but every time she has slipped away and eventually the trail runs cold.

Currently, as an agent of the Rose and Raven Society, I have been working with Seth Aubrey to chronicle the story of Sabastian Wolfram. I shall write about that account when we have completed the task. In the meantime, should you be interested in The Rose and Raven Society, there is a manual with accounts, rules, and regulations of the society available if one knows where to look.

My advice to you is to beware of the night, for there are more things in this world than you have dreamed of in your lifetime.

www.ingramcontent.com/pod-product-compliance
Lightning Source LLC
LaVergne TN
LVHW041610070526
838199LV00052B/3081